Abortion

by Wendy Lanier

LUCENT BOOKS

A part of Gale, Cengage Learning

Detroit • New York • San Francisco • New Haven, Conn • Waterville, Maine • London

LIBRARY OF CONGRESS CATALOGING-IN-PUBLICATION DATA

Lanier, Wendy, 1963–
  Abortion / by Wendy Lanier.
    p. cm. — (Hot topics)
  Includes bibliographical references and index.
  ISBN 978-1-4205-0116-2 (hbk.)
  1. Abortion—United States—Juvenile literature. I. Title.
  HQ767.5.U5L365 2009
  363.460973—dc22

                                                          2008052819

Lucent Books
27500 Drake Rd.
Farmington Hills, MI 48331

ISBN-13: 978-1-4205-0116-2
ISBN-10: 1-4205-0116-X

Printed in the United States of America
1 2 3 4 5 6 7 13 12 11 10 09

CONTENTS

FOREWORD

Young people today are bombarded with information. Aside from traditional sources such as newspapers, television, and the radio, they are inundated with a nearly continuous stream of data from electronic media. They send and receive e-mails and instant messages, read and write online "blogs," participate in chat rooms and forums, and surf the Web for hours. This trend is likely to continue. As Patricia Senn Breivik, the former dean of university libraries at Wayne State University in Detroit, has stated, "Information overload will only increase in the future. By 2020, for example, the available body of information is expected to double every 73 days! How will these students find the information they need in this coming tidal wave of information?"

Ironically, this overabundance of information can actually impede efforts to understand complex issues. Whether the topic is abortion, the death penalty, gay rights, or obesity, the deluge of fact and opinion that floods the print and electronic media is overwhelming. The news media report the results of polls and studies that contradict one another. Cable news shows, talk radio programs, and newspaper editorials promote narrow viewpoints and omit facts that challenge their own political biases. The World Wide Web is an electronic minefield where legitimate scholars compete with the postings of ordinary citizens who may or may not be well-informed or capable of reasoned argument. At times, strongly worded testimonials and opinion pieces both in print and electronic media are presented as factual accounts.

Conflicting quotes and statistics can confuse even the most diligent researchers. A good example of this is the question of whether or not the death penalty deters crime. For instance, one study found that murders decreased by nearly one-third when the death penalty was reinstated in New York in 1995. Death

4

penalty supporters cite this finding to support their argument that the existence of the death penalty deters criminals from committing murder. However, another study found that states without the death penalty have murder rates below the national average. This study is cited by opponents of capital punishment, who reject the claim that the death penalty deters murder. Students need context and clear, informed discussion if they are to think critically and make informed decisions.

The Hot Topics series is designed to help young people wade through the glut of fact, opinion, and rhetoric so that they can think critically about controversial issues. Only by reading and thinking critically will they be able to formulate a viewpoint that is not simply the parroted views of others. Each volume of the series focuses on one of today's most pressing social issues and provides a balanced overview of the topic. Carefully crafted narrative, fully documented primary and secondary source quotes, informative sidebars, and study questions all provide excellent starting points for research and discussion. Full-color photographs and charts enhance all volumes in the series. With its many useful features, the Hot Topics series is a valuable resource for young people struggling to understand the pressing issues of the modern era.

THE ABORTION
DEBATE IN AMERICA

The issue of abortion could easily be the most hotly debated topic of the previous century. Prior to the 1970s all elective abortions in America were illegal, a fact that did not stop many women from seeking to have one. In the early 1970s, after hearing the now famous *Roe v. Wade* case, the Supreme Court declared laws preventing early-term abortions unconstitutional in the United States for the first time.

The Supreme Court's decision paved the way for legal abortions and unleashed a firestorm of controversy over moral and legal obligations to women and unborn children. Many people took the position of defending the rights of the unborn and became part of the pro-life movement. Many others believed a woman should have the right to choose whether to carry a baby to full term or not. These people became part of the pro-choice movement.

For the past several decades, people on both sides of the issue have continued to debate the question of whether legal abortions should be made available to women and to what point in their pregnancy. At times the debate has turned violent. Angry clashes between pro-life and pro-choice demonstrators have resulted in property damage, fights, abortion clinic bombings, and even murder. Feelings run high among extremists on both sides.

Now, well into the twenty-first century, the questions remain. There is no one pro-life or pro-choice position. Different terms have different definitions among different groups. New technology has made earlier detection of pregnancy possible.

At the same time new options for early abortions have become available. These factors have ultimately created more questions without providing any answers.

The abortion issues of today are mainly about parental notification, partial birth abortions, and the extent to which states may limit abortion access. While the *Roe v. Wade* Supreme Court decision of 1973 made abortion legal, it also gave the states the power to restrict access to abortion on a state level. Because of this, abortion services vary greatly from state to state. Some states require parental notification or permission for minors, while others do not. All states have varying amounts of mandatory counseling prior to abortion services as well as a specified waiting period. And some states allow late-term abortions, while others have strict limits on abortions after certain points in the pregnancy.

The abortion debate sparks strong feelings in both the pro-life and pro-choice camps.

Why Women Get Abortions

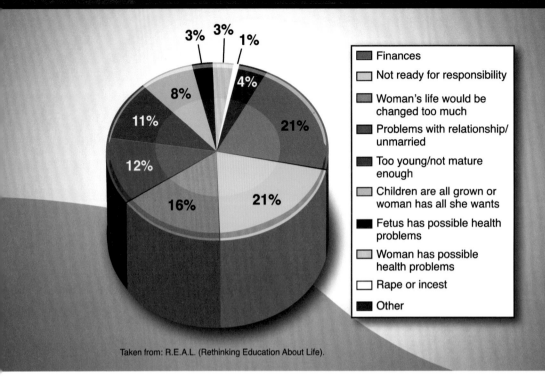

Legend:
- Finances
- Not ready for responsibility
- Woman's life would be changed too much
- Problems with relationship/ unmarried
- Too young/not mature enough
- Children are all grown or woman has all she wants
- Fetus has possible health problems
- Woman has possible health problems
- Rape or incest
- Other

3% 3% 1% 4% 8% 11% 12% 16% 21% 21%

Taken from: R.E.A.L. (Rethinking Education About Life).

Since the U.S. Supreme Court's *Roe v. Wade* decision, there have been many attempts to pass laws regulating abortion access. Political groups on both sides of the abortion issue have established powerful lobbies in an effort to influence the outcome of elections. Political candidates find the question of abortion to be a minefield they sometimes try to avoid. At times the outcome of an election has been determined by a candidate's stance on this one issue.

The questions surrounding the abortion issue are many and complex. Is abortion a moral solution to an unwanted pregnancy? What right, if any, does the government or anyone else have to limit abortion access to a woman who is pregnant? The answers are often not as straightforward as they may first appear.

Is Abortion Moral?

At the heart of the abortion issue is the question of morality. As people struggle with the question of whether abortion is right or wrong, many factors come into play. Religious beliefs, age, marital status, economic status, health, an available support system, genetic issues, and a person's own values all influence the way he or she feels about abortion. For a woman who may be considering such a procedure, the decision takes on an extremely personal nature as her own circumstances weigh heavily in her private debate.

In giving careful thought to the morality of abortion, two additional questions are often raised. At what point does life begin? And at what point do the rights of this developing life (if ever) overrule the rights of the mother? The answers have produced a range of feelings on the issue.

It Begins at the Beginning

"Human life begins at conception. That is not a religious posture, but a scientific fact that the lowest paid laborer on the planet can assert without qualm. What we do with that understanding is another matter." —Kathleen Parker, syndicated columnist.

Kathleen Parker, "Human Life Begins at Conception," KansasCity.com, 2008. www.kansascity.com/273/story/776096.html.

Pro-Life Position

For most pro-life groups and conservative Christians, the answer to the question of when life begins is—at conception. A fertilized ovum, or zygote, contains forty-six chromosomes in a DNA structure different from either the sperm or ovum that joined to create it. It is able to grow and reproduce on its own, uses energy, and reacts to stimuli. People who believe that abortion is immoral in all or most cases argue that a fertilized ovum is a new and unique human life with all the rights of any other

Pro-life groups believe that life begins at conception, and that abortion, therefore, kills a human being.

human. In support of this view, Albert W. Liley, an often-quoted physiologist known as the "Father of Fetology," observes: "Biologically, at no stage of development can we subscribe to the view that the unborn child is a mere appendage of the mother. Genetically, the mother and baby are separate individuals from conception."[1]

Those who view human life as beginning at conception give the same value to a zygote as they would a newborn. Any effort to prevent further development of the zygote to the pre-embryo stage is viewed by them as the destruction of human life. In this case even the use of emergency contraceptives (also known as the "morning-after" pill) could be considered a type of abortion since it does not allow the zygote to implant itself into the wall of the uterus. While the morning-after pill may act as a contraceptive if taken before ovulation, the Association of Prolife Physicians and other pro-life groups take the position that when taken during or after ovulation it is "not contraceptive because it does not prevent conception, but rather, this aborts the life of a week-old human being."[2]

In general, pro-life advocates believe it is wrong to abort an embryo or fetus because it is not wanted or the mother is uncertain of her ability to care for it. In their view the government should intervene to require a woman to continue her pregnancy to childbirth in many or all cases, with few exceptions.

PRO-LIFE ON THE MORALITY OF ABORTION

"Legality is not morality. . . . It has been legal to murder an unborn baby in America for the last 30 years. . . . But morality is eternal, and regardless of the current state of the law, such actions will always be immoral." —Vox Day, author and opinion columnist.

Vox Day, "R.I.P Connor Peterson," WorldNetDaily. www.wnd.com/news/article. asp?ARTICLE_ID=32267.

Special Circumstances

Although pro-life advocates believe abortion is wrong, many Americans believe abortion is acceptable in some circumstances.

In 2006 former South Dakota state representative Jan Nicolay (right) and representative Elaine Roberts (second from the right) introduced a petition drive to put South Dakota's abortion ban on the ballot. The ban—the strictest abortion law in the United States—made exceptions only to save the mother's life, excluding special circumstances like rape or incest.

Polls over the past decade show many people, including some pro-life supporters, do not believe a woman should have to endure any pregnancy caused by rape or incest. In addition, it is generally felt a pregnancy that endangers the life or long-term health of the mother should be terminated. A 2008 Gallup poll indicated 54 percent of Americans believe abortions should be legal only under these special circumstances. Because they believe these circumstances are beyond a woman's control, most people believe abortion is a moral option in these cases.

Some pro-life supporters are willing to make allowances for these special circumstances because they believe them to be rare. Research suggests such circumstances occur less than 7 percent of the time. In the pro-life view, only a small fraction of the abortions carried out in the United States each year are for acceptable reasons.

Pro-Choice Position

The basic pro-choice position centers on the belief that the life of the fetus should not be given more consideration than the rights of the mother. Pro-choice advocates believe a woman's reproductive rights include access to sex education, the right to choose a safe, legal abortion, access to contraceptives, and the power to control her own body. They do not believe the government should be able to interfere with a woman's decision to have an abortion at all.

Those with a pro-choice viewpoint see abortion as a private medical decision that should be made by a woman and her doctor without government interference. They are opposed to any legislation regarding abortion for fear it could lead to forced abortions, an idea they find just as offensive as the laws limiting its access. Canadian author Joyce Arthur writes: "People often refer to anti-choice and pro-choice as 'two sides.' In fact, the anti-choice are in favour of forced motherhood, and the opposite of that is forced abortion. We oppose both of these extremist positions."[3]

When Does Life Begin?

Scientists at the U.S. Department of Energy's Ask a Scientist Web site were asked the question, when does life begin? Steve J. Triezenberg gave this response:

This is an important topic, but even (or especially) for a scientist you and I must realize that my "moral beliefs" will affect the kind of answer I give.

Even the unfertilized egg and sperm are "alive" so in some sense life begins before fertilization! The fertilized egg is certainly alive, in that it can copy its genetic information (DNA) and it can divide into more and more cells. The more critical question, I think, is when that life becomes "human," and that is not a question that science will be able to answer. Humanness is a religious, or moral, or philosophical question that is not likely to have a single agreed upon answer.

Quoted in Ask a Scientist, U.S. Department of Energy, "When Does Life Begin?" www.newton.dep.anl.gov/askasci/bio99/bio99189.htm.

In her 1999 remarks to the National Abortion Rights Action League (now known as NARAL Pro-Choice America), Hillary Clinton voiced the pro-choice viewpoint by saying, "Being pro-choice is trusting the individual to make the right decision for herself and her family, and not entrusting that decision to anyone wearing the authority of government in any regard."[4]

IT'S ALIVE, BUT IS IT HUMAN?

"If we're talking about life in the biological sense, eggs are alive, sperm are alive. Cancer tumors are alive. For me, what matters is this: When does it have the moral status of a human being? When does it have some kind of awareness of its surroundings?" —Bonnie Steinbock, professor of bioethics and philosophy.

Quoted in ReligiousTolerance.org, "When Does Human Personhood Begin?" www.religious tolerance.org/abo_argu.htm.

In addition to situations involving rape, incest, or life/health issues for the mother, pro-choice advocates believe there are other situations in which an abortion might be a moral choice. They believe, for example, a woman whose contraceptive failed or who feels unable to raise a child given her personal circumstances should have access to a safe, legal abortion if she chooses. Margaret Sykes, a pro-choice view spokesperson for AllExperts.com, believes that "having an abortion is not a life-changing decision for anyone. Becoming a mother is, for more than one person."[5] Pro-choice supporters argue that when safe, legal abortions are available, larger numbers of children who are born will be wanted by their parents. This, they believe, ultimately reduces the number of children in foster care due to abuse and neglect.

Many pro-choice organizations choose to focus their attention on reducing the number of unwanted pregnancies through comprehensive sex education in high schools, the use of contraceptives, and greater parental involvement. In their view, limited sex education programs without instruction in the use of contraceptives actually increases the demand for abortions rather than decreasing it. They believe abstinence-only programs favored by the pro-life groups are unrealistic and fail to address the current permissive attitude toward sexual activity among teens. George Monbiot of a British newspaper, the *Guardian*, says, "The most effective means of preventing the deaths of unborn children is to promote contraception."[6]

Pro-choice supporters often express frustration with pro-life groups because they believe they ignore many of the social ills

Those with a pro-choice viewpoint believe that the government should not interfere with a woman's decision regarding whether or not to have a baby.

Adoption: A Moral Alternative?

Pro-life advocates frequently tout adoption as the moral solution to an unwanted pregnancy. They believe adoption offers a way of escape for a reluctant parent without destroying an embryo. Pro-life groups such as the Center for Life and Hope advise their prospective clients that adoption can give women the freedom to pursue their goals and know they have made a caring decision for their child. There are many young couples that cannot have their own children and are waiting to adopt a child.

Pro-choice supporters, however, do not necessarily see adoption as a moral choice. To many pro-choice individuals, adoption carries as much responsibility as parenting but without the control. Sociologist and author of the 1984 classic *Abortion and the Politics of Motherhood* Kristin Luker makes it clear that having a baby and giving it up for adoption is not seen by most pro-choice people as a moral solution. Pro-choice supporters believe that to transform a fetus into a baby and then send it out into the world where the parents can have no assurance it will be well loved and cared for is the height of moral irresponsibility.

created by children who are unwanted or whose parents are unable to care for them adequately. This view is voiced by British biologist Michael J. Tucker when he says, "If the anti-abortion movement took a tenth of the energy they put into noisy theatrics and devoted it to improving the lives of children who have been born into lives of poverty, violence, and neglect, they could make a world shine."[7]

In general, pro-choice groups consider the morality of abortion to be a private decision based on personal circumstances. For many, however, there is a point at which the developing fetus must be given some consideration.

Question of Personhood

Many pro-choice individuals believe the mother's rights override those of the fetus because they believe the fetus does not become a human being until sometime after conception. Until then they believe the mother's reproductive rights and the right to control her own body supersede any rights of the fetus. While they do not argue with the idea life begins at conception, they differ from those with a pro-life view in assigning the same value to the zygote as to a newborn.

Peter Singer, a Princeton ethicist, believes all human life is not equal. He says:

> The pro-life groups are right about one thing, the location of the baby inside or outside the womb cannot make much of a moral difference. We cannot coherently hold it is alright to kill a fetus a week before birth, but as soon as the baby is born everything must be done to keep it alive. The solution, however, is not to accept the pro-life view that the fetus is a human being with the same moral status as yours or mine. The solution is the very opposite, to abandon the idea that all human life is of equal worth.[8]

While some pro-choice advocates believe abortion should be an available option at any time in a woman's pregnancy, many others believe it should be an option only until the stage at which a fetus becomes a human being. In a 2008 *Time* poll, 46 percent of the respondents felt abortion should be legal for any reason in the first three months. This response may indicate they believe "personhood" to be achieved sometime soon afterward.

Pro-Choice on the Morality of Abortion

"The true morality of abortion lies in the informed consent of the pregnant woman. . . . It is immoral to force a woman to carry to term or have an abortion regardless of the circumstances surrounding her pregnancy." —Kelly Gorski, author, communications editor, and former pregnancy options counselor.

Kelly Gorski, "Lacking Morality of the Pro-Choice Argument," EzineArticles.com. http://ezinearticles.com/?Lacking-Morality-of-the-Pro-Choice-Argument&id=74132.

At what point personhood occurs is not clearly defined, but many markers have been proposed. It might be when the embryo's heart starts beating, when it first looks human, when

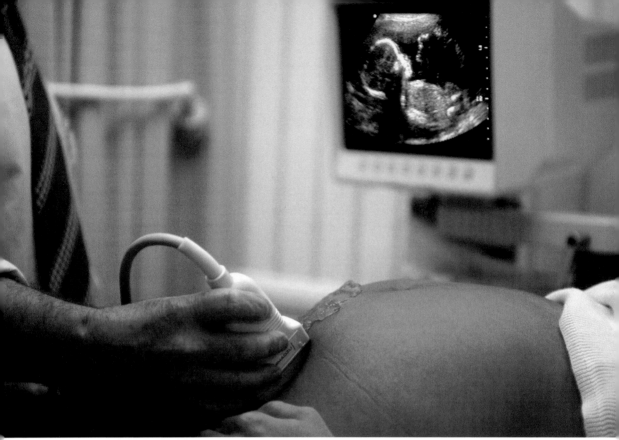

At the core of the abortion debate is the seemingly unanswerable question "When does life begin?"

it becomes aware of its surroundings, at quickening (the point when the mother can feel the movement of the fetus), or at the point the fetus is viable outside the womb and could survive, if necessary, apart from its mother. The lack of agreement about personhood is largely what makes it difficult to pinpoint a definitive pro-choice viewpoint on this aspect of the abortion issue.

Personal Morality Versus Public Morality

Because there are so many opinions about when life begins and at what point it must morally be preserved, it is unlikely there will be agreement any time soon. Political parties, politicians, and abortion interest groups will continue their debate. And every day, decisions will continue to be made about abortion on a personal level. These decisions are intensely private. What a person may say in public about abortion may differ from how they view it for themselves.

For a number of years now, polls have consistently shown most Americans (more than half) have no desire to overturn the *Roe v. Wade* decision of 1973. Americans, in general, appear to believe abortion should remain legal and be left to the discretion of a woman and her doctor throughout some or all of the gestation period. When a 2007 national poll asked Americans if they supported the Supreme Court's *Roe v. Wade* decision, 56 percent answered yes.

A different answer, however, is often given when pollsters ask a slightly different question. When asked if they believe abortion to be right or wrong, almost half of those surveyed said they thought it was wrong. Another 10 percent said it depended on the circumstances. This is a surprising revelation, considering most Americans believe abortion, at least in some cases, should be legal. Most people appear to believe abortion is wrong on a personal level, but are convinced others should be free to make a different choice for themselves.

In 2006 researchers at Hamilton College in Clinton, New York, conducted a poll of high school seniors nationwide. Working with the polling firm of Zogby International, researchers found most students (66 percent) regard abortion as always or almost always morally wrong and would severely limit a woman's right to choose. The same study, however, revealed over 60 percent believe the *Roe v. Wade* decision should stand and abortion should remain legal, giving women the right to choose.

The morality question is apparently one the majority of Americans consider to be a private decision. They are reluctant for government to have any part of it. Even many of those who are morally opposed to abortion feel making it illegal would lead to unsafe back-alley procedures, ultimately resulting in serious women's health issues. With the loss of what they view as a personal freedom at the hands of their government, they fear that losing other personal freedoms would be inevitable.

Tim Johnson is a medical editor for ABC News who appears regularly on the ABC network to explain medical and health issues. He finds that he, like so many other Americans, is of two

The morality issues surrounding abortion make it a very difficult decision for a woman facing an unexpected pregnancy.

minds when it comes to the issue of abortion. "I find myself saying that I am anti-abortion but also pro-choice. I do find the idea and act of abortion distasteful or even offensive. And I recognize that it destroys a life in the making. But . . . I support the right of each woman to decide what is the right choice for her."[9]

Clearly, the abortion debate rages not only on a national and political level, but on a very personal one as well. Journalist Anna Quindlen sums it up by saying, "And that is where I find myself now, in the middle—hating the idea of abortion, hating the idea of having them outlawed."[10] Many people recognize her dilemma and share her frustration.

More than thirty-five years after the legalization of abortion, Americans are still struggling with both their private feelings and the legal aspects of this topic. Is abortion moral? On a personal level the decision is a very private one, influenced by religious beliefs, marital or economic status, available resources, health, and many other considerations. Publicly, however, the morality of abortion is likely to continue to be a point of debate for years to come.

IS ABORTION A CONSTITUTIONAL RIGHT?

Laws regarding abortion existed long before the independence of the United States. In 325 B.C. ancient philosopher Aristotle decreed, "The line between lawful and unlawful abortion will be marked by the fact of having sensation and being alive."[11] This quickening was the basis for most laws on the matter for the past two thousand years.

Before *Roe v. Wade*

At the time of U.S. independence, the only laws on abortion were those of common law (adopted from England and based on legal decisions of the past). Common law favored Aristotle's idea of abortion being acceptable as long as it occurred before quickening. James Wilson, one of the authors of the Constitution, a lawyer, and one of the original justices on the Supreme Court, expressed the views of the Founding Fathers in a paper entitled *Of the Natural Rights of Individuals*. In it he wrote: "In the contemplation of law, life begins when the infant is first able to stir in the womb. By the law, life is protected . . . from every degree of danger."[12]

By the 1820s anti-abortion laws began to appear in various states. During this time Connecticut passed a law aimed at stopping the sale of poisons to women for abortion purposes. A few years later New York made post-quickening abortions a felony. In the late 1800s the trend toward making abortion illegal continued to gain momentum, and by 1900 abortion at any stage of pregnancy was illegal in most states, although some did allow the practice under limited circumstances.

The fact that abortions were illegal, however, did not stop them from occurring. Illegal abortions continued to be available for those who had the means to afford them. The Guttmacher Institute estimates two hundred thousand to 1.2 million illegal abortions a year were performed from 1950 to 1970. These procedures were often unsafe and sometimes resulted in death. In 1965 about two hundred women died from complications of

Eighteenth-century illustration showing the concept of "quickening," the time when the first fetal movements are felt by the mother, typically sixteen to eighteen weeks after conception.

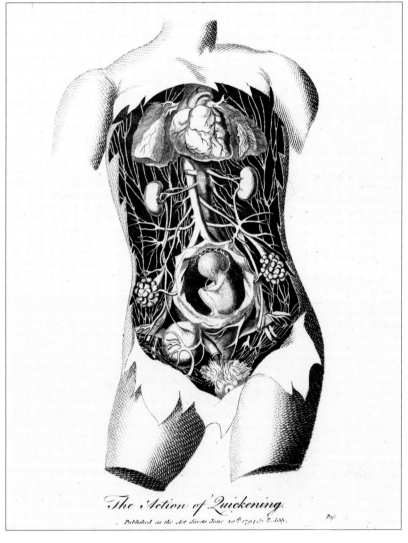

The Action of Quickening.

Published as the Act directs June 10th 1791 by E. Sibly.

an illegal abortion. The fear of unsafe abortion procedures and the belief that they should be made readily available led some groups to provide secret abortion services.

One of the best-known examples was a group of women in Chicago who operated a floating (always moving) abortion clinic in the 1960s. Known as "JANE," the clinic originally worked with doctors who performed abortions by making arrangements for women to have the procedure done in secret. As the demand grew, the creators of JANE learned to perform abortions themselves in order to meet the demand. Between 1969 and 1973 the members of JANE assisted with or performed an estimated eleven thousand illegal abortions.

AT WHAT POINT DOES A HUMAN HAVE A RIGHT TO LIFE?

"Whether you're looking at it from a theological perspective or a scientific perspective, answering that question with specificity is above my pay grade." —Barack Obama, senator.

Quoted in *Time*, "McCain and Obama on Abortion," August 17, 2008. www.time.com/time/nation/article/0,8599,1833496,00.html.

What *Roe v. Wade* Did

By the beginning of the 1970s, some states were beginning to legalize abortion for situations involving rape or incest and for cases in which the woman's life or health were endangered by her pregnancy. Other states adopted less restrictive laws allowing abortions for reasons other than for these extreme cases. This caused significant differences in abortion regulations from state to state.

In 1969 a twenty-two-year-old Texas woman named Norma McCorvey was devastated to learn Texas was one of the states in which abortions were still illegal except in cases where the mother's life was in danger. Pregnant with her third child, McCorvey desperately tried to find an abortion provider but was unsuccessful. Instead she became the plaintiff in a landmark lawsuit challenging the Texas law prohibiting abortion and took on the pseudonym "Jane Roe" to protect her identity. At the time, McCorvey did not realize any victory in the case would come too late to allow her to have an abortion. Long before the case reached the Supreme Court, McCorvey's child had been born and given up for adoption.

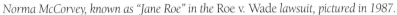

Norma McCorvey, known as "Jane Roe" in the Roe v. Wade *lawsuit, pictured in 1987.*

In 1973 the U.S. Supreme Court ruled on the case that came to be known as *Roe v. Wade*. In its ruling the Court stated that women, upon the advice and counsel of their doctors, had a constitutional right to have an abortion in the early stages of pregnancy. The justices stated that a first trimester embryo was not a person under the Constitution and a woman's right to privacy included the right to an abortion. They further determined the states could intervene in second trimester abortions and outlaw them altogether in the third except in cases where the woman's life or health was at risk.

In a separate decision regarding *Roe v. Wade*'s companion case, *Doe v. Bolton*, the Court ruled threats to a woman's health could be physical, emotional, psychological, her age, or familial (family related). This broad definition allowed any licensed

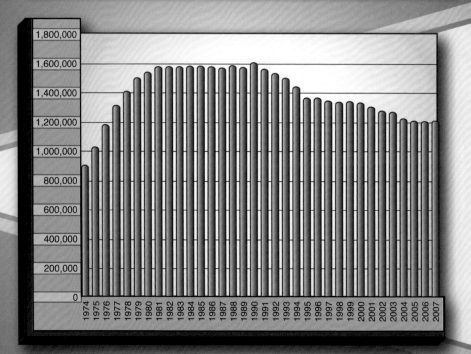

Abortion Rates in the United States

Taken from: R.E.A.L. (Rethinking Education About Life).

physician willing to perform an abortion the legal option to do so. By 1983 a Senate Judiciary Committee evaluated the status of abortion rights in America and concluded that "no significant legal barriers of any kind whatsoever exist today in the United States for a woman to obtain an abortion for any reason during any stage of her pregnancy."[13]

In the wake of the Supreme Court's decision, the number of legal abortions rose sharply and continued to a peak of about 1.6 million in 1990. Beginning in the early 1990s, the number began slowly to decline. By 2005 the number had fallen to 1.21 million. The Guttmacher Institute estimates more than 45 million legal abortions have been performed in the United States since 1973.

A QUESTION OF RELIGION

"Whether or not abortion should be legal turns on the answer to the question of whether and at what point a fetus is a person. The concept of personhood . . . is essentially a religious, or quasi-religious idea, based on one's fundamental (and therefore unverifiable) assumptions about the nature of the world." —Paul Campos, professor of law at the University of Colorado.

Quoted in ReligiousTolerance.org, "When Does Human Life Become a Human Person?" www.religioustolerance.org/abo_when.htm.

Planned Parenthood v. Casey

The Supreme Court did not revisit the issue of abortion again until 1992, when it heard the case of *Planned Parenthood v. Casey*. The decision in this case upheld a woman's right to an abortion as part of her liberty and privacy protected by the Fourteenth Amendment. However, due to advancements in medical technology, the Court also determined a fetus might be considered viable as early as twenty-two to twenty-three weeks (instead of the previous twenty-eight weeks). Their decision struck down the trimester formula of *Roe v. Wade* and allowed states to impose restrictions after viability so long as they did not create an "undue burden" for women seeking abortion.

The Fourteenth Amendment

Citizens of this country enjoy personal privacy based on something implied in civil law but not explicitly stated. The Fourteenth Amendment (one of three Civil War amendments) gave citizenship to former slaves freed by the Thirteenth and given the right to vote by the Fifteenth.

Over the years protections in the Bill of Rights (the first ten amendments to the Constitution) have been incorporated into the due process section of the Fourteenth Amendment. This clause asserts that no authority may deprive a citizen of the United States of "life, liberty or property" without due process (valid law applied in a proper fashion). In recent years protection of privacy, particularly in a person's home or body, has been added to the many specific protections given by the Bill of Rights (freedom of speech, worship, etc.).

The most controversial decision handed down based on this implied right is found in *Roe v. Wade*. In *Roe* the Supreme Court placed a woman's decision to have an abortion under the seal of privacy protected by the Constitution. And while abortion is not formally permitted by the Constitution, the decision to undergo the procedure is a protected activity.

Partial Birth Abortion Ban

Beginning in 1995 the U.S. Congress made several attempts to pass federal laws banning a particular type of abortion—intact dilation and extraction. Also known as partial birth abortion, this procedure is a type of late-term abortion. President Bill Clinton vetoed bills in 1996 and 1997 on the grounds that they did not include health exceptions. When a similar bill containing an exemption to allow the procedure if a woman's life was threatened was passed, President George W. Bush signed it into law in 2003. The law was immediately challenged. By the fall of 2006, the case had found its way to the Supreme Court. In 2007 the Supreme Court upheld the nationwide ban, ruling it did not conflict with previous Court decisions. The partial birth abortion ban became the first federal legislation to limit abortion in any fashion since 1973.

Where Are We Now?

As of January 2009 in the United States, women of all ages may undergo legal abortion through about twenty-four weeks of pregnancy. After twenty-four weeks most states have limits, except in cases where a woman's life or health is at risk. In addition, many abortion providers choose not to perform late-term abortions (which may be considered to be as early as sixteen weeks).

President George W. Bush signs the Partial-Birth Abortion Ban Act of 2003.

ABORTION NOT A CONSTITUTIONAL RIGHT

"Abortion could never be a protected constitutional right simply because granting rights to one party (the mother) automatically cancels out the rights of the other (the unborn child). The Constitution . . . [has] never restricted the rights of one group in order to grant rights to another." —Barry Ready, conservative political blogger.

Barry Ready, "Abortion Not a Constitutional Right," Palmetto Pundit, November 14, 2005. http://palmettopundit.blogspot.com/2005/11/abortion-not-constitutional-right.html.

While abortion is legal in all fifty states, each state has the right to establish restrictions that do not create an "undue burden" for women seeking them. This means they may not enact restrictions that serve no legitimate purpose, would cause difficulty in receiving abortion services, or impose excessive expense. The most common restrictions today are parental notification or consent requirements for minors, state-sponsored counseling and waiting periods, and limitations on public funding.

The 1973 Supreme Court decision established abortion as a constitutional right, protected by the Fourteenth Amendment. Justice Harry Blackmun, who wrote the majority opinion for *Roe v. Wade*, noted, "The right of privacy . . . is broad enough to encompass a woman's decision whether or not to terminate her pregnancy."[14] His fellow justice, Byron White, however, did not agree. In his dissent he wrote, "I find nothing in the language or history of the Constitution to support the Court's judgment."[15]

Pro-Life Views on Constitutional Rights

Pro-life advocates do not believe abortion is a right guaranteed by the Constitution. Instead they point out that because the Constitution is silent on the subject, the current basis for abortion rights is an implied right subject to the interpretation of the Court. In a widely read 1984 essay titled *Abortion and the Conscience of the Nation*, President Ronald Reagan voiced the pro-life viewpoint by saying: "Make no mistake, abortion-on-demand is not a right granted by the Constitution. No serious scholar, including one disposed to agree with the Court's result, has argued that the framers of the Constitution intended to create such a right."[16]

Pro-life supporters believe a woman's right to privacy and control of her own body stops at the point where it affects a life other than her own. In their view the developing fetus is another person completely separate from the mother, dependent on her only for food and shelter—just as if it were already born. They believe the rights of all individuals must be considered, including those of persons who are not yet born.

Pro-life advocates are convinced abortion devalues human life prior to birth and could lead to the devaluation of human life at other stages. If a human fetus has no rights, they argue, who

A pro-life demonstrator dresses as George Washington during a right-to-life demonstration in front of the U.S. Supreme Court. Pro-life advocates do not believe that the founding fathers intended to protect abortion in the Constitution.

A pro-choice sign showing a crossed-out coat hanger, symbolizing the primitive and dangerous methods women used to terminate pregnancies before the legalization of abortion.

will be next? Will some future society determine other members of society to be of no value and therefore unnecessary? By allowing abortion on demand, pro-life advocates believe a dangerous precedent is being established that might one day lead to the destruction of handicapped individuals, the elderly, the homeless, or some other segment of society labeled as unwanted or unnecessary.

Pro-Life Arguments for Overturning *Roe v. Wade*

Pro-life advocates believe the 1973 *Roe v. Wade* (and *Doe v. Bolton*) should be overturned. They cite the language of the Constitution itself, and the Fourteenth Amendment in particular, as the basis for protecting the life of the unborn. They believe the framers of the Constitution had the unborn in mind when they declared their intent to "secure the blessings of liberty to ourselves and our posterity" in the preamble. They believe these words identify the unborn as worthy of the same right to "life, liberty, and the pursuit of happiness" as any other American.

Many pro-life supporters also believe the general public is unaware of the extent to which abortion is currently available in the

United States. Due, in part, to opinion polls in recent years, many pro-life supporters are convinced the American public does not support abortion on demand. They believe the public has been misled into believing *Roe v. Wade* allows abortions only under limited circumstances, and the majority would be unwilling to make them available wholesale if the decision were left to the voters. Pro-life advocates support overturning *Roe v. Wade* completely in favor of new legislation defining clear limits on abortion that they believe would better reflect the will of the people.

Pro-Choice Views on Constitutional Rights

Those with a pro-choice viewpoint see the question of constitutional rights from a completely different angle. They believe a woman's right to privacy and reproductive control are protected by the Fourteenth Amendment. On the basis of this amendment, the 1965 case of *Griswold v. Connecticut* determined that liberty included the concept of personal privacy. Pro-choice supporters believe this encompasses a woman's right to make her own reproductive decisions, including whether to carry a fetus to term or to have an abortion. In their view any limitations placed on abortion access are a clear violation of constitutional rights.

Aside from the question of rights, pro-choice advocates also have a fear of having the religious or philosophical beliefs of a single group forced on everyone. While many pro-choice individuals acknowledge abortion is not the best option for everyone, they believe the decision is a private one to be made by a woman with the counsel of her doctor or other medical adviser.

Right to an Abortion

"Access to safe abortion is both a fundamental human right and central to women's health. Where abortion is illegal or inaccessible, the search for abortion humiliates women and undermines their self-respect and dignity." —Zanele Hlatshwayo and Barbara Klugman, South African Women's Health Project.

Quoted in the Pro-Choice Public Education Project, "Abortion Rights and Reproductive Justice." www.protectchoice.org/article.php?id=130.

It is not, they argue, a decision that should be subject to public opinion or philosophy.

Pro-Choice Arguments in Favor of *Roe v. Wade*

As far as pro-choice supporters are concerned, *Roe v. Wade* should stand as is. They believe the ensuing legal restrictions of the last decade have rendered the 1973 decision less effective. Pro-choice advocates strongly believe in the Supreme Court's original decision—that a woman's right to privacy extends to her decision to abort an unwanted pregnancy if she chooses to do so. Overturning *Roe v. Wade* to make abortion illegal once again would serve no constructive purpose, they argue, since studies have shown making it illegal does not have any impact on the number of abortions actually performed. "Evidence from

Abortion Time Line

1973: The Supreme Court, in *Roe v. Wade*, grants women the right to terminate pregnancies through abortion. The ruling is based on a woman's right to privacy. In a separate case, *Doe v. Bolton*, the Supreme Court votes 7-2 to invalidate a Georgia law that required a woman to get approval from three physicians before having an abortion.

1976: Congress passes the Hyde Amendment, banning the use of Medicaid and other federal funds for abortions. The legislation is upheld by the Supreme Court in 1980 but amended by Congress in 1994 to allow Medicaid to pay for abortions in cases of rape or incest or to save the life of the mother.

1981: In *Bellotti v. Baird*, the Supreme Court rules that pregnant minors can petition a court for permission to have an abortion without parental notification.

1992: In *Planned Parenthood v. Casey*, the Court reaffirms *Roe*'s core, holding that states may not ban abortions or interfere with a woman's decision to have an abortion. The Court does uphold mandatory twenty-four-hour waiting periods and parental-consent laws.

2003: Congress passes the Partial-Birth Abortion Ban Act of 2003, which includes a provision to protect a woman's health. The Supreme Court upholds the ban in 2007.

around the world shows that placing restrictions on abortion to make it harder to obtain has much more to do with making it less safe than making it rarer,"[17] says Susan Cohen, director of government affairs at the Guttmacher Institute.

Illegal abortions, pro-choice supporters point out, are still abortions. Making them illegal would only result in "underground" services such as the ones prior to 1973. This, they fear, would likely be unsafe and allow opportunists to take advantage of women at a time when they are most vulnerable. They believe a ban on abortions would ultimately cause much harm to women's individual health and their health care in general.

Current Attitudes Toward Legality of Abortion

Along with their questions about the morality of abortion, Americans struggle with the question of whether or not abortion should remain legal. Their convictions about what is wrong, however, do not always lead to the conclusion that abortion should be illegal.

Current opinion polls show Americans will continue to support legal abortions, although most appear to be uncomfortable with abortion on demand. Less than 20 percent believe abortion should be available with no restrictions. More than half say abortion should be legal only under certain circumstances. No one, it seems, is eager to return to the days of back-alley abortions in less-than-safe surroundings. Instead Americans cautiously endorse legal abortions as an option they hope will be less needed as time goes on.

CHAPTER 3

MORE ABORTION QUESTIONS

Current surveys indicate Americans favor legal abortions but not in all circumstances. Some of the situations about which they have reservations involve late-term abortions or women under the age of eighteen. As Americans learn more about abortion options and fetal development, they are more inclined to form opinions about abortion limits and availability.

ABSURD NOTION

"The method of killing a human child . . . proscribed by this statute is so horrible that the most clinical description of it evokes a shudder of revulsion. . . . The notion that the Constitution of the United States . . . prohibits the states from . . . banning [it] is quite simply absurd." —Antonin Scalia, Supreme Court Justice.

Antonin Scalia, dissenting opinion, *Stenberg v. Carhart*, 530 U.S. 914 (2000).

A Growing Awareness

In the years before *Roe v. Wade*, Americans were generally uneducated about matters relating to sexuality and childbirth. Many of the topics discussed openly in today's society were considered taboo. Types of birth control were limited and not readily available, especially for the very poor or the very young.

Today the general public is more informed about birth control, abortion, and fetal development. Due to scientific advancements the number of birth control and abortion options has greatly increased. Many of the mysteries of child development in the womb have been revealed through modern technology.

Americans expressing an opinion today are far more likely to have an informed opinion than they were thirty-five years ago.

In addition to a better-educated public, advances in the field of medicine are making it possible for infants to survive outside the womb as early as twenty-two weeks. This possibility is causing some to rethink their position on late-term abortions.

Late-Term Abortions

The label "late term" as it applies to abortion is the source of some disagreement. There is no medical definition for the point at which an abortion becomes late term. Some consider late term to be after the first trimester, which is twelve weeks. Others set the limit at sometime during the second trimester, usually after sixteen or twenty weeks. Late-term abortions are generally performed when a medical abortion (induced using medications or

Abortion Counseling

All states require health care providers to obtain consent from patients prior to a nonemergency medical procedure. As a matter of routine, the provider must give their patients information on the procedure, its risks, and any alternative treatments. For abortions, however, the manner and extent of this information is a source of disagreement between pro-life and pro-choice supporters.

Currently, thirty-three states have some law or policy related to informed consent for abortion. In ten of these states, the information provided includes a description of the procedure to be performed and the gestational age of the fetus. In twenty-three states, providers are required to make information available in oral and written form and must explain about the specific procedure the woman is about to undergo. Some of these states include information about procedures not being provided as well. In eight of the twenty-three states, the law requires the provider to inform a woman seeking an abortion that her decision must be strictly voluntary. Thirteen states have a requirement related to ultrasound, a practice criticized by pro-choice supporters as unnecessary before a first trimester abortion. In addition, states must provide information about potential risks—also criticized by pro-choice groups as often inaccurate.

via means of vacuum aspiration) is no longer possible. Late-term procedures are much more invasive and present a greater risk to the pregnant woman.

About 90 percent of all abortions performed in the United States each year occur during the first twelve weeks of pregnancy, while second trimester abortions account for about 9 percent of the yearly total. In many of the second trimester cases, the woman either did not realize she was pregnant or was in denial about her condition until she was obviously pregnant. In a few circumstances ultrasound or amniocentesis revealed a potentially serious genetic defect in the fetus or the pregnancy was determined to be ectopic. Ectopic pregnancies occur when the fertilized egg implants outside the uterus, usually in the fallopian tubes. This is a serious health risk to the mother and certain death for the fetus.

In less than 1 percent of the abortions performed each year, the procedure is delayed until the third trimester. Most states have laws limiting abortions after the twenty-fourth week except in cases where the fetus is already dead, the mother's life or health is seriously at risk, or in cases of rape or incest. Of the approximately 1.2 million abortions performed in the United States each year, about twelve thousand occur during the third trimester. Third trimester abortion options are limited to induced labor, hysterotomy, and intact dilation and extraction, also known as a partial birth abortion.

The most common of these procedures is the intact dilation and extraction. Physicians who perform later-term abortions often prefer it because there is no chance of leaving any part of the fetus in the womb, which reduces the chance of infection. The procedure is generally considered easier to perform than the others.

What Are Partial Birth Abortions?

Introduced by Martin Haskell in the early 1990s as an improvement over the dilation and evacuation method, intact dilation and extraction (D&X) is usually performed on women who are between twenty and twenty-four weeks pregnant or in the third trimester. During the procedure the doctor delivers all but the head of the fetus from the uterus, and then uses scissors to cut a hole in the base of the fetus's skull so its contents can be removed. This causes the fetus's head to collapse, allowing it to pass through the cervical opening more easily.

C. Everett Koop, former surgeon general of the United States, has denounced D&X procedures as unprofessional. He believes no competent physician with state-of-the-art skill in the management of high-risk pregnancies needs to perform a D&X. While the American College of Obstetricians and Gynecologists agreed there were no circumstances under which a D&X was the only option, they also determined "an intact D&X . . . may be the best or more appropriate procedure in a particular circumstance to save the life or preserve the health of a woman, and only the doctor, in consultation with the patient, based on the woman's particular circumstances can make this decision."[18]

Representative Randy Ball (R-MN) holds up a pair of scissors used in partial birth abortions, 1999. He sponsored a bill that year to outlaw partial birth abortions.

WHAT IS AT STAKE?

"Of course it's a horrible procedure. No one would argue with that. But if your life is at stake, if your health is at stake, if the potential for having any more children is at stake, this must be a woman's choice." —Hillary Clinton, senator and former First Lady.

Hillary Clinton, Senate debate in Manhattan, October 8, 2000.

Why Pro-Choice Advocates Support Partial Birth Abortions

Pro-choice advocates say they support partial birth abortions primarily as a means of protecting the life of a pregnant woman. They believe a woman whose life is at risk has a greater right to life than the developing fetus and are convinced a D&X involves less risk to the woman than other procedures. In their view when an abortion is determined to be in the best interest of the life and health of a woman, the decision about the type of procedure to be used should rest entirely with the woman and her doctor.

Pro-choice supporters are quick to point out that D&X procedures are only used in rare cases under extreme circumstances. They refer to current statistics that show less than 10 percent of the abortions performed each year are done after the twelfth week and only a fraction of those are D&X procedures. Pro-choice advocates believe circumstances such as a woman's life or health being at risk, a dead or severely deformed fetus, or a serious genetic defect justify a D&X abortion.

Why Pro-Life Supporters Object

Pro-life supporters are passionately opposed to D&X abortions. They believe them to be barbaric and unnecessary even in cases where the mother's life may be at risk. Instead they advocate early delivery as a means of saving the mother's life. Because pro-life advocates believe the developing fetus has the same right to life as the mother, they believe whatever steps are necessary should be taken to preserve the life of the fetus as well. To them, D&X abortions are infanticide, or the killing of an infant.

In addition, pro-life groups are dubious about claims that D&X procedures are rare and only performed in extreme circumstances. They point to statements from leading abortionists who tell a different story. For example, in a 1993 interview with the *American Medical News,* Martin Haskell said, "I'll be quite frank: Most of my abortions are elective in that 20 to 24 week range . . . 80 percent are purely elective."[19] Dr. Haskell has indicated that his preferred method of abortion at this stage is D&X. Due to statements like this, pro-life supporters believe D&X procedures are more frequently used as a method of birth control than the general public is willing to support. They believe there are no circumstances under which the procedure is an acceptable practice.

Should Partial Birth Abortions Be Banned?

The partial birth abortion ban of 2003 was the first federal legislation to have a significant impact on abortion laws since *Roe v. Wade* and *Doe v. Bolton.* Upheld by the Supreme Court in 2007,

Nebraska physician Leroy Carhart challenged state and federal bans on partial birth abortions.

Other Abortion Laws

Physician and Hospital Requirements: 38 states require abortions to be performed by a licensed physician. 19 states require an abortion to be performed in a hospital after a specified point in the pregnancy. . . .

Public Funding: 17 states use their own funds to pay for all or most medically necessary abortions for Medicaid enrollees in the state. 32 states and the District of Columbia prohibit the use of state funds except in those cases when federal funds are available: where the woman's life is in danger or the pregnancy is the result of rape or incest. In defiance of federal requirements, South Dakota limits funding to cases of life endangerment only. . . .

State-Mandated Counseling: 17 states mandate that women be given counseling before an abortion that includes information on at least one of the following: the purported link between abortion and breast cancer (6 states), the ability of a fetus to feel pain (8 states), long-term mental health consequences for the woman (7 states) or information on the availability of ultrasound (6 states).

Waiting Periods: 24 states require a woman seeking an abortion to wait a specified period of time, usually 24 hours, between when she receives counseling and the procedure is performed.

Excerpted from Guttmacher Institute, "State Policies in Brief: An Overview of Abortion Laws." www.guttm acher.org/statecenter/spibs/spib_OAL.pdf.

the partial birth abortion ban prohibits the procedure unless necessary to save the life of the mother. This might be when a woman's life is endangered by a physical disorder, physical illness, or physical injury and provided there is no other medical procedure that will suffice. Under this law the performance of a partial birth abortion can result in a fine or imprisonment up to two years or both. It also provides for civil action by the father and maternal grandparents of the fetus. And it prohibits the prosecution of a woman on whom a partial birth abortion is performed.

Although not a topic of extensive debate in recent years, poll results in 2003 and 2007 show Americans are in favor of partial birth abortion bans by a wide margin. Even those who are willing to allow for a serious health-risk exception still feel the procedure should be illegal in most cases.

Abortion Laws from State to State

Although abortion is legal in the United States, certain restrictions have been put into place, leading to variations in abortion laws from state to state. In its 1992 *Planned Parenthood v. Casey* decision, the Supreme Court upheld the legality of abortion but gave individual states the right to restrict abortion access as long as they did not create an "undue burden" on women. This gave states the right to restrict abortion or prohibit it entirely after viability except when necessary to protect the woman's life or health. Nearly all states currently have some type of legislation that affects abortion access or its cost.

As of July 2008 state laws on abortion include a variety of restrictions. Thirty-six states prohibit abortion after fetal viability except when necessary to protect a woman's life or health. In addition, thirty-eight states require an abortion to be performed by a licensed physician, and nineteen states require an abortion to take place in a hospital after a specified point in the pregnancy. Abortion counseling is mandated in seventeen states and may include information about a possible link between abortion and breast cancer, the ability of the fetus to feel pain, possible long-term mental health consequences for the woman, or the availability of ultrasound. Additionally, there are twenty-four states that require a waiting period (usually twenty-four hours) between the time of abortion counseling and the time the procedure is performed.

CONSISTENCY OF THE LAW

"If a parent has the right to stop his or her children from tattooing or piercing their own bodies, it seems ridiculous that they do not also have the right to review the child's decision to have a much more invasive operation performed." —Sarah Hargrove, Vanderbilt University.

Sarah Hargrove, "Abortion: Is Parental Consent Necessary?" *Orbis*, October 15, 2003. http://media.www.vanderbiltorbis.com/media/storage/paper983/news/2003/10/15/UndefinedSection/Abortion.Is.Parental.Consent.Necessary-2471656.shtml.

Should Parental-Consent Laws Be Mandatory?

Along with the restrictions listed above, thirty-five states have laws requiring parent involvement at some level for women who are under the age of eighteen. Some states require parental consent, while others only require they be notified of the procedure before it takes place. In twenty-two states a minor must have the permission of one or both parents before she can legally have an abortion. There are eleven states that require one or both parents to be notified of the procedure, and two states require both parental consent and notification.

Recent polls indicate Americans overwhelmingly favor parental notification, with only a slightly smaller percentage willing to take the restriction a step further and require parental consent. Overall, about 70 percent of Americans support consent laws. This number includes Republicans, Democrats, independents, and young people (ages eighteen to twenty-nine).

To take into account special circumstances, most states have enacted judicial bypasses in which a pregnant teen can ask a judge to allow her to have an abortion without telling or receiving consent from her parents or legal guardian. The judge can grant the request if he or she believes the teen is mature enough and sufficiently well informed to make the decision for herself, if notification of a parent or guardian would cause the teen to be harmed in some way, or if the notification of the parent or guardian is not in the best interest of the minor. The hearing to determine whether the judge will allow an abortion without parental consent or notification is usually confidential.

MORE HARM THAN GOOD?

"While the intent of such laws is to enhance family communication, the failure to guarantee confidentiality often deters young people from seeking timely services and care resulting in increased instances of sexually transmitted diseases, unwanted pregnancies, and late term abortions." —The American Association of University Women.

Quoted in Auriana Ojeda, "Should Abortion Rights Be Restricted?" eNotes.com. www.enotes.com/should-abortion-article/39731.

Three women hold signs protesting Texas governor Rick Perry's signing of a bill in 2005 that requires minors to get written parental consent for abortions.

Opposition to Parental-Consent Laws

Pro-choice advocates oppose parental-consent laws as unnecessary since most minors tell one or both parents anyway. Studies indicate about 60 percent voluntarily involve their parents. For those who are afraid to tell because of abuse by a family member, however, pro-choice groups worry they may resort to illegal abortions or simply travel to nearby states with fewer restrictions in an effort to avoid further abuse.

Pro-choice supporters are not convinced judicial bypass procedures are the solution in these cases due to significant inconsistencies among states. Margaret Sykes, who writes for AllExperts.com on pro-choice views, has suggested some states approve all requests while others approve none. On this subject she points out:

> In 1990, when the Supreme Court was deciding the constitutionality of Minnesota's parental notification law, one

of the groups opposing the law was the judiciary of Minnesota. All the judges who testified, who had heard 3000 or so bypass requests from minors and who were both pro-choice and pro-life, agreed the law was a travesty. They testified unanimously that it was "useless, cruel, and a detriment to family harmony."[20]

In addition, pro-choice supporters believe a double standard exists in the area of parental consent. In most states a minor may choose to carry her baby to term, place it for adoption, and make decisions about her prenatal and delivery care, all without the consent or knowledge of her parents. Choosing to end the pregnancy, they argue, is no different. They believe forcing a pregnant minor to obtain parental consent sets a standard that clearly favors one resolution over another and restricts the choices of young women.

Support for Parental Consent

Those who support parental-consent laws argue that minors are required to have parental approval for most medical procedures, including dental work, flu shots, or even the dispensing of an aspirin at school. They believe parental consent should also include decisions related to pregnancy or abortion. They point out that parents are legally responsible for minors and would incur any medical expenses due to complications from the abortion if any should arise. They also worry complications could go untreated or misdiagnosed if parents are unaware an abortion has taken place.

In general, young people seem to agree with parental-consent laws. A 2005 Gallup poll indicated 69 percent supported such laws. There was almost no difference between the eighteen to twenty-nine age group response and that of the other age groups.

Hard Questions, Hard Choices

The abortion debate is clearly not a matter of a simple yes or no. There are many questions surrounding the issue that require individual scrutiny. Decisions about these individual questions often

Pennsylvania mother Joyce Farley speaks out in favor of laws requiring minors to get parental consent before receiving an abortion. Her daughter traveled to a different state to get an abortion without her permission.

result in conflicting answers. Americans who support abortion rights may be opposed to late-term abortions. Pro-life supporters sometimes find themselves taking pro-choice stands, while pro-choice individuals are sometimes surprised to find themselves in agreement with a pro-life view. The questions about abortion are complex and difficult to answer. Forming an opinion or making a decision requires making hard choices.

CHAPTER 4

DOES ABORTION HAVE LONG-TERM EFFECTS?

Another aspect of the abortion debate is the controversy over whether having the procedure results in long-term health consequences. Ordinarily a simple search of the Internet would provide the answers. In the case of abortion, however, there are two separate schools of thought. People on both sides of the issue have formed opinions based on what they may believe to be scientific evidence. Sometimes the "evidence" is actually biased information or based on case studies rather than random samples. Although there is no lack of information dedicated exclusively to the topic of abortion, the method of collecting the information as well as its source must be carefully considered.

THE RIGHT THING

"Even if no solid evidence provides a causal link to increased rates of depression . . . , abortion is often a grim event. . . . You don't have to be . . . anti-abortion . . . to feel sorrow over an abortion, or to be haunted about whether you did the right thing."
—Emily Bazelon, author, editor, and journalist.

Emily Bazelon, "Is There a Post-Abortion Syndrome?" *New York Times,* January 21, 2007. www.nytimes.com/2007/01/21/magazine/21abortion.t.html?pagewanted=3.

Problems with Information About Abortion's Effects

Many pro-life supporters are firmly convinced there are dramatic consequences to abortion. Pro-life Web sites and counseling centers usually offer long lists of possible side effects ranging from discomfort to bleeding to death. Many of the complications they mention can and do happen, but they are rare. The incidence of severe complications or death is nominal compared to the number of abortions performed annually.

It is difficult to assess accurately the number of deaths or complications because there are no requirements for states to report abortion data to any federal agency. Current figures do not include results for several states, including California, the most populous state. In spite of this, the Guttmacher Institute estimates the death rate associated with abortion is one in 1 million at or before eight weeks. The number rises, however, to one per twenty-nine thousand at sixteen to twenty weeks, and one per eleven thousand at twenty-one weeks or more.

Pro-choice advocates insist abortion is safe. This is generally true, but abortion service providers sometimes downplay possible complications or fail to provide adequate information about what happens during the procedure. Women who ask questions

Female patient advocates answer questions by phone at an abortion provider in 1994.

about the appearance of the fetus or how much discomfort they can expect may be given incomplete or false information. Sometimes this is an effort to spare the woman's feelings. In some cases, however, it is done to ensure the woman will go through with the abortion.

During the thirty-five-plus years abortion has been legal, a number of studies have been done in an effort to determine what, if any, long-term conditions may occur as a result of abortion. Such studies have looked at a variety of possible conditions, including breast cancer, infertility, miscarriages, and post-abortion depression. The results have not always provided conclusive answers.

Is There a Link Between Abortion and Breast Cancer?

Many pro-life supporters believe abortion causes abrupt hormonal changes that can lead to breast cancer in later life. Over the years studies of women with breast cancer seemed to indicate a higher incidence of prior abortion. However, because the samples in the studies only included women with cancer, researchers were unable to select random samples to minimize false results.

In order to produce more reliable results, it would be necessary to determine the incidence of prior abortions among the same number of women without breast cancer. But some researchers have suggested women who are healthy are less likely to reveal a previous abortion. This could make it appear as though women who have had an abortion have a higher incidence of breast cancer, even though the frequency between the two groups may actually be the same.

Beginning in the mid-1990s, results from more reliable studies became available for the first time. A Danish study completed in 1997 included every Danish woman born between April 1935 and March 1987—about 1.5 million women. Because the studies took the women's entire medical history into account, the results were considered more reliable. Researchers found no direct link between induced abortion and breast cancer. They did find a slightly increased risk for those who had late-term abortions, but

Illinois state senator Pat O'Malley testifies during a Senate committee hearing on whether there is a link between abortion and breast cancer.

cautioned the numbers involved were too small to be significant. Further study of late-term abortions is needed to verify or disprove any relation between the two.

By 2003 the Committee on Gynecological Practice made the following observation: "Early studies of the relationship between prior induced abortion and breast cancer risk have been inconsistent and are difficult to interpret because of methodological considerations. More rigorous recent studies argue against a causal relationship between induced abortion and a subsequent increase in breast cancer risk."[21]

Since the publication of the Danish study, additional research has served to support its results. The Collaborative Group on Hormonal Factors, established in 1992, collects data from studies around the world for evaluation. In 2004 the Collaborative Group on Hormonal Factors in Breast Cancer evaluated the information

A Pro-Life Perspective on Abortion's Effects

Based on the results of a comprehensive women's health study that reviewed over sixty international studies and included over 1 million women, Elizabeth Shadigian and her colleagues determined that:

Abortion Increases the Risk of:
- Breast cancer—the protective effect of a full-term pregnancy is lost when a woman has an abortion; by itself abortion slightly increases the risk of breast cancer.
- Depression and suicide—increased depression; women who have had an abortion are twice as likely to harm themselves, attempt suicide, or commit suicide.
- Pre-term birth and placenta previa—increased risk of premature babies or placenta previa (cervix is blocked by the placenta, requiring a C-section) in later pregnancies.

Abortion Does Not Increase the Risk of:
- Infertility
- Miscarriage
- Tubal or ectopic pregnancy

in fifty-three separate studies, including eighty-three thousand women from sixteen countries that allow abortion. They reported no increase in a woman's risk of breast cancer due to miscarriage or induced abortion.

Not all researchers, however, are completely convinced. A 2003 study conducted by a team of physicians from the University of North Carolina School of Medicine reviewed more than sixty international studies including more than 1 million women. Their findings, published in the *Obstetrical and Gynecological Survey*, indicated the completion of a full-term pregnancy provides a measure of protection against breast cancer that is lost when a woman has an abortion. They believe the occurrence of an abortion creates a slightly elevated risk for breast cancer later in life. In summarizing their findings, the team noted, "Women contemplating their first induced abortion early in their reproductive life should be informed . . . they will lose the protective effect of a full-term delivery on their lifetime risk of breast carcinoma."[22]

Does Abortion Cause Infertility or Miscarriages?

Most researchers agree today's abortion procedures carry only a small risk of causing damage that would lead to infertility or miscarriage. Generally, abortions in the first trimester are non-surgical procedures that do not require cervical dilation or the scraping of the uterus to remove traces of pregnancy tissue. These types of abortions carry only slight risks such as might be expected with any medical procedure, especially if they are carried out in a hospital setting.

NO RISK TO MENTAL HEALTH

"Most women do not experience psychological problems or regret their abortion 2 years post abortion, but some do. Those who do tend to be women with a prior history of . . . depression. . . . Thus, for most women, elective abortion of an unintended pregnancy does not pose a risk to mental health." —Brenda Major, professor of psychology.

Brenda Major et al., "Psychological Responses of Women After First-Trimester Abortions," *Archives of General Psychiatry*, August 2000. www.archpsy.ama-assn.org/cgi/content/full/57/8/777.

The later an abortion is performed, the more intrusive it is for a woman's body. Any procedure that dilates the cervix can weaken it. In addition, the cleaning of the uterus can cause scarring. Multiple abortions tend to increase these factors, which can lead to the inability to carry a pregnancy to term in later attempts. In order to minimize this possibility, a woman who wishes to become pregnant after having one or more abortions should consult with her physician, who can determine whether scarring or a weakened cervix is a potential problem. As long as an abortion is performed by a competent physician in a reputable hospital or clinic setting, the chances of being left infertile or miscarrying a future pregnancy are very slight.

Studies have shown a very small risk of infertility after an abortion.

Can Complications Result from an Abortion?

Because abortion is a medical procedure, there is always a chance of complications. While pro-life groups may tend to exaggerate the dangers in trying to persuade women not to have abortions, the opposite can be true of pro-choice groups. Although the risks of having a legal abortion are very small, for some women the resulting complications can be life-changing.

The most common complications resulting from an abortion include pain, excessive bleeding, tearing or puncture of the uterus, cervical damage, or infection. If the physician fails to remove all tissue associated with the pregnancy, the woman can develop a severe infection known as sepsis. All of these conditions are treatable but can lead to serious health issues and even death if left untreated. The Guttmacher Institute estimates 0.3 percent of patients (about 3,600) experience complications serious enough to require hospitalization each year. However, there is no way to know how many of the hundreds of infections reported for women of childbearing age annually might be related to abortion, which would have an effect on the Guttmacher estimate.

The complications mentioned above are much less frequent in abortions performed at less than six weeks of pregnancy. However, the percentage climbs sharply after the first trimester. The most common complications in the second and third trimesters are cervical injuries, excessive bleeding, and infection. The safest abortions are nonsurgical procedures that are carried out as early in the pregnancy as possible.

Approximately 0.3 percent of abortion patients must be hospitalized for treatment of complications each year, although this number may be much higher.

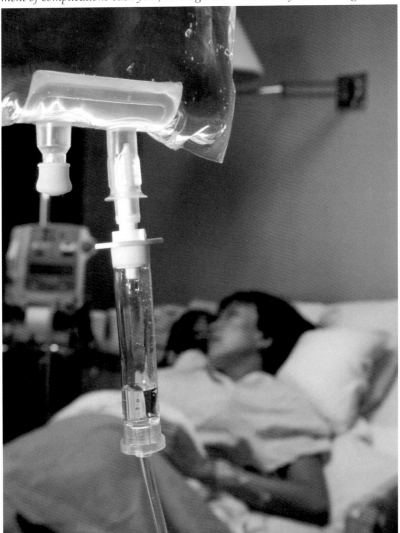

ABORTION MAY BE ASSOCIATED WITH MENTAL HEALTH PROBLEMS

"The findings suggest that abortion in young women may be associated with increased risks of mental health problems. . . . It is our view that the issue of whether or not abortion has harmful effects on mental health remains to be fully resolved." —David M. Fergusson, professor, Christchurch School of Medicine and Health Sciences.

David M. Fergusson et al., "Abortion in Young Women and Subsequent Mental Health," *Journal of Child Psychology and Psychiatry*, 2006. www.chmeds.ac.nz/research/chds/view1.pdf.

Are There Long-Term Psychological Effects From Abortion?

The decision to have an abortion is not an easy one. Any unplanned pregnancy and the circumstances accompanying it put a woman under tremendous stress. During this stressful and complicated time, she must make a decision that has the potential to affect the rest of her life. Her choices are limited—carry the baby to term and take on the responsibility of raising a child, carry the baby to term and place it for adoption, or abortion. Once a woman makes a decision, she must be willing to live with it. There is no going back.

For some women the emotional aspects of abortion linger long after the procedure is done. Post-abortion syndrome (PAS) is rare but can be a serious problem for women who are haunted by their decision. It mainly affects women who were pressured into an abortion they did not want, those who believed at the time of the abortion they were ending the life of a human being, or those who changed their beliefs about abortion after the fact. While the occurrence of PAS is statistically very low, women who fall into one of these categories may experience debilitating bouts of depression, anxiety, drug abuse, or suicidal episodes months or even years after their abortion.

In 1987 surgeon general C. Everett Koop was directed by President Ronald Reagan to prepare a report on the health effects of abortion. Koop, a vocal abortion opponent, gave the matter careful study over a fifteen-month period. Ultimately, he concluded the psychological effects of abortion to be minuscule

Women carry signs reading "I Regret My Abortion" during a march outside of the U.S. Supreme Court Building on the anniversary of the Roe v. Wade *decision that legalized abortion.*

from a public health perspective. In his report Koop also noted the lack of scientifically sound research to make a direct connection between abortion and mental health. Psychological problems in the wake of an abortion may or may not be a result of the abortion. They may, instead, be reflective of the factors surrounding the unwanted pregnancy or the mental stability of the woman before she became pregnant. Either way, Koop noted, "obstetricians and gynecologists had long since concluded that the physical sequelae [aftereffects] of abortion were no different than those found in women who carried pregnancy to term or who had never been pregnant."[23]

Despite Koop's findings and subsequent studies that support them, pro-life supporters believe PAS is a common and frequently occurring side effect of abortion. Many pro-life Web sites provide checklists of behaviors they believe are associated with the aftereffects of the decision to abort. Some organizations cite a frequency of PAS symptoms as high as 60 percent.

IS THERE A LINK?

"I entered this study with no preconceived conclusion. . . . This [post-abortion syndrome] appears to be rare, contrary to the beliefs of many pro-lifers. But it does exist, contrary to the beliefs of many pro-choicers. When it does occur, it can be profoundly debilitating." —Bruce A. Robinson, author and coordinator of ReligiousTolerance.org.

Bruce A. Robinson, "Overview: Do Abortions Trigger Later Emotional or Physical Health Problems?" ReligiousTolerance.org. www.religioustolerance.org/abohealth.htm.

In 2006 the results of a five-year study by the University of Oslo showed negative psychological effects associated with abortion five years after the procedure. The study included eighty women who had abortions and forty who had suffered miscarriages. The women were given several questionnaires ten days, six months, two years, and five years after the event.

A Pro-Choice Perspective of Abortion's Effects

In the last 30 years, researchers have considered the long-term implications of terminating a pregnancy. And despite challenges in all stages of the research process—from study design, through data collection and analysis, to the interpretation of results—the preponderance of evidence from well-designed and well-executed studies indicates that abortion is safe over the long term and carries little or no risk of fertility-related problems, cancer or psychological illnesses.

- Abortion does not impair a woman's future fertility
- Abortion is not associated with an increased risk of cancer
- Abortion does not pose a hazard to a woman's mental health

Heather Boonstra et al., *Abortion in Women's Lives*, Guttmacher Institute, 2006, pp. 22–24. www.guttmacher.org/pubs/2006/05/04/AiWL.pdf.

At the ten-day point, 48 percent of the women who had miscarriages were suffering distress, while only 30 percent of those who had aborted indicated any emotional trauma. By the end of the five years, however, only 2.6 percent of the women who had suffered miscarriage were still showing signs of distress, compared to 20 percent of those who had an abortion.

Many pro-choice advocates do not believe PAS exists, or if they do, they believe the effects of PAS to be minimal. It is possible that because they believe this, they tend to downplay the possibility of future emotional suffering due to PAS. Susan Cohen of the Guttmacher Institute voices the pro-choice sentiments on PAS by saying, "It is fair to say that neither the weight of the scientific evidence to date nor the observable reality of 33 years of legal abortion in the United States comports with the idea that having an abortion is any more dangerous to a woman's long-term mental health than delivering and parenting a child that she did not intend to have or placing a baby for adoption."[24]

No matter how a woman may feel about abortion or its possible consequences, just wading through all the conflicting information can be daunting. As one young woman put it:

> "Never in my time of having this procedure done did anyone go over the aftereffects of what this procedure can do to you mentally. . . . I know that this will be with me till my dying day and I have to accept that to be able to get through this. . . . By no means am I saying to have an abortion is wrong or right I just think that there should be a little more honesty involved in it."[25]

Any woman who chooses to have an abortion should be aware of the possible consequences of her decision. Although risks are slight, they do exist. Most women do not experience serious complications but for those who do, the decision to abort can be hard to live with.

VOICES OF EXPERIENCE

Any woman who has had or ever considered having an abortion has a story to tell. Some are stories of triumph, while others are filled with pain. For every woman who experiences one of the more than 3 million unintended pregnancies each year, there is a difficult choice to be made. Once the decision is made, it cannot be changed.

WHAT MIGHT HAVE BEEN

"Don't ever delude yourself with the hoax that abortion is a quick, painless solution. . . . The grief of 'What my child could have been, if only I had let him live . . .' will last forever." —Jennifer, personal story.

Quoted in Larry Davies, "Abortion: A Personal Story," Sowing Seeds of Faith. www. sowingseedsoffaith.com/abortion.htm.

Toughing It Out

In spite of difficult circumstances, some women ultimately choose not to abort. As a nineteen-year-old black woman attending college in the 1950s, Barbara was a rarity. Her brains and drive were taking her places many young black women did not have the opportunity to go. Her future was bright with promise.

When Barbara discovered she was pregnant, her mother insisted she have an abortion. She was certain having a baby would end Barbara's quest for an education and her chance to make her mark on the world.

In spite of Barbara's misgivings, she was taken to a chiropractor who was also known to handle abortions. Lying on the table being prepped for the procedure, Barbara dissolved into tears. The chiropractor gave her a long look and asked her a defining question. Did she want to keep the baby? When Barbara nodded through her tears, the man took her mother aside and talked her into taking Barbara home.

The years that followed were difficult at best. Barbara's grandmother kept her daughter while Barbara attended college, graduated, and began teaching. Barbara studied hard in school and worked several jobs to meet expenses. Eventually, she became a successful school principal and a savvy businesswoman. The daughter she almost aborted is a chemical engineer, author, and speaker who has been a source of joy and pride for over fifty years.

Single women who decide to go through with an unplanned pregnancy often face significant emotional and economic challenges.

Looking back, Barbara says: "Those were hard times. There were days when we didn't have anything to eat but soup. But I wouldn't trade them for anything. When I look at my daughter now—I see a miracle. I am so proud of all that she has already accomplished, and I know she's just getting started. I am so grateful I chose not to end her life. Look what I would have missed!"[26]

TRAPPED?

"[A woman does not want an abortion] like she wants a Porsche or an ice cream cone. Like an animal caught in a trap, trying to gnaw off its own leg, a woman who seeks an abortion is trying to escape a desperate situation by an act of violence and self-loss." —Frederica Mathewes-Green, author, feminist, and pro-life activist.

Frederica Mathewes-Green, "Abortion: Women's Rights . . . and Wrongs," Feminists for Life. http://feministsforlife.org/FFL_topics/after/rtnwrfmg.htm.

No Regrets

According to the most recent figures available, in 2005 more than 1.2 million legal abortions were performed in the United States. Many of those decisions were made by women who have no regrets. They believe the quality of their lives is better because a safe, legal abortion was available to them.

When thirty-two-year-old Alexandra, the mother of two boys, became pregnant due to failed contraceptives, it could not have come at a worse time. Although she and her husband were both working, they were having trouble making ends meet. To make matters worse, Alexandra was battling severe depression. With no money for professional help, a full-time job, and two little boys to parent, Alexandra chose to abort her pregnancy. She believed then, as now, that her primary responsibility was to her sons, her husband, and herself.

Alexandra notes:

Eight years later, I still have no regrets—only an ever-strengthened belief that what I did was the right thing to do at the time. I am still extremely happily married. We are financially stable. My two children are healthy and happy. They have a mother that has dealt with her depression and is a very happy woman these days. All these things would never have happened, I am convinced, had I not made the decision for an abortion eight years ago.[27]

Some women have no regrets about their abortion, believing that it allowed them to be better mothers when they decided to have children.

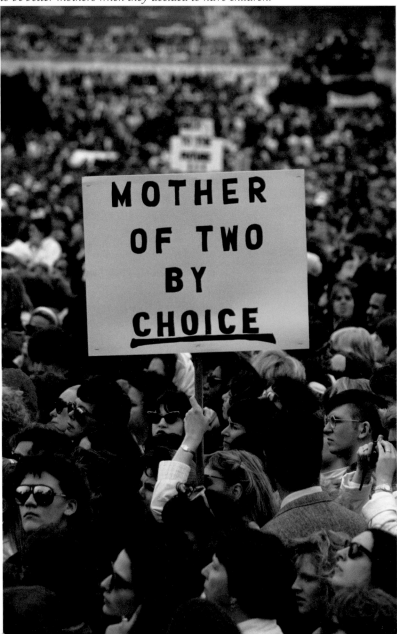

Haunted

For women who allow someone else to pressure them into having an abortion or cannot quite convince themselves it is the right thing to do, the abortion experience is usually less than positive. Failure to deal with whatever a woman may be feeling at the time can lead to years of frustration.

In 1973 Deborah was a fifteen-year-old teen living in what appeared to outsiders as a typical American family. On the inside her blue-collar father was distant at best, and her mother was dealing with issues of her own. The verbal and psychological abuse she experienced drove Deborah into rebellion. As part of her attempts to assert herself, she began dating an older boy who was eighteen. After their first sexual encounter, she became pregnant. The day Deborah found out, the boy left town. In thirty-five years Deborah has never seen or heard from him again.

When Deborah's parents learned she was pregnant, they made it clear she would have an abortion. There would be no discussion. If she chose not to go along with their decision, she would be thrown out of their house. They were more concerned about appearances and what people would think than about Deborah. Terrified, she gave in.

Although Deborah's mother drove her to the women's clinic where the abortion was performed, she did nothing to prepare Deborah or support her in any way. Deborah remembers that the clinic staff talked with her about the machinery that would be used and described the procedure for her in "soft" terms she did not really understand. There was nothing in their explanation about what would happen to her physically or how it would affect her emotionally. There was no discussion of Deborah as a person or how she felt about things. No one asked her if she wanted the abortion.

Ironically, even though parts of the experience are sketchy for Deborah after thirty-five years, the memory of the procedure itself is crystal clear. She says:

> I remember every second of the actual procedure. The whole thing was very uncomfortable and the dilation of my cervix hurt—a lot. I could hear the noise of the vacuum and feel them moving it around inside me. I couldn't

run a vacuum cleaner for years after that. I just could not make myself do it. I was awake for the whole thing. There was a clinic worker who stood near my head and patted me and told me it was going to be alright.[28]

With the ordeal behind her, Deborah's mother drove her home. Deborah spent her recovery time alone in her room. There was no follow-up counseling—in fact, Deborah's parents never mentioned it again—ever. It was difficult for Deborah to process. She felt as though she was running from something constantly. She realizes her abortion was only a part of the whole picture, but she feels it is what pushed her to become more promiscuous and into substance abuse and eventually a half-hearted attempt to kill herself at sixteen. She was convinced she was worthless. For years she continued on a path of self-destruction.

The executive director (right) and a volunteer counselor outside of a Crisis Pregnancy Center in Washington, D.C.

Incidence of Abortion in the United States

- Nearly half of pregnancies among American women are unintended, and four in 10 of these are terminated by abortion. Twenty-two percent of all pregnancies (excluding miscarriages) end in abortion.
- Forty percent of pregnancies among white women, 69% among blacks and 54% among Hispanics are unintended.
- In 2005, 1.21 million abortions were performed, down from 1.31 million in 2000. From 1973 through 2005, more than 45 million legal abortions occurred.
- Each year, about two percent of women aged 15–44 have an abortion; 47% of them have had at least one previous abortion.

Who Has Abortions?
- Fifty percent of U.S. women obtaining abortions are younger than 25: Women aged 20–24 obtain 33% of all abortions, and teenagers obtain 17%.
- Thirty-seven percent of abortions occur to black women, 34% to non-Hispanic white women, 22% to Hispanic women and 8% to women of other races.
- Forty-three percent of women obtaining abortions identify themselves as Protestant, and 27% as Catholic.
- Women who have never married obtain two-thirds of all abortions.
- About 60 percent of abortions are obtained by women who have one or more children.

Excerpted from Guttmacher Institute, "Facts on Induced Abortion in the United States," July 2008. www.guttmacher.org/pubs/fb_induced_abortion.html.

Finally, at the age of thirty-seven, Deborah participated in a seven-week counseling program through Crisis Pregnancy Centers. Through the program she was able to work through her feelings about her abortion and reach a place of peace. She says:

> I had to get to a point where I could humanize the aborted fetus, accept what I had done, and forgive myself. I had been angry and depressed all the time, but I'm emotionally ok with it now. It is part of who I am. I am not tormented any more. It took me until I was 37, but I made it. My kids tell me I act like a kid sometimes. I tell them I'm just having fun—I missed that kid thing the first time around.[29]

Grateful for the Choice

At twenty-two Christy was about to do something no one in her family had ever done before—graduate from college. Her hard work was about to pay off.

When her contraceptive methods (birth control pills and condoms) failed, however, Christy was faced with a big decision. Her family and her boyfriend put enormous pressure on her to carry the baby to term in spite of Christy's desire to have an abortion. Everyone promised to help. "I felt trapped," she says, "and buried under the weight of their promised generosity, the guilt they leveled onto me for 'even considering' abortion and what they thought was 'support.'"[30]

Since no one offered to help with the cost of an abortion, Christy's decision was delayed until it was too late. She was forced to carry her pregnancy to term. Her son was born two weeks after she turned twenty-three. Soon after, her support began to evaporate as both her family and her boyfriend failed to deliver on their promises. Her boyfriend even quit his job to work for under-the-table wages so he would not have to pay child support. Christy was left to deal with motherhood with little support.

ABORTION REFLECTION

"It's been three years since my abortion, and after a lot of emotional processing one of the main feelings I'm left with is . . . gratitude. . . . I feel like the experience has made me . . . stronger. . . . I look forward to choosing to have a baby." —Anonymous.

Quoted in Feministing.com, "What Makes for a Good Abortion?" http://community.feministing.com/2008/07/what-makes-for-a-good-abortion.html.

With her mother's help, Christy managed to get a tiny apartment near the university and continue her education. By 2006 she was working two jobs, taking graduate classes at night, and trading off babysitting with a group of mothers in her apartment complex. She was dating again and using the birth control patch, but she had difficulty keeping it in place. Before she could get to the health center to switch to the pill, she discovered she was pregnant.

This time Christy resolved things would be different. Even though she loved her son, allowing herself to be pressured into having him was a decision she still regretted. She had no desire to repeat the trauma she had experienced in pregnancy, childbirth, and as a new mother. She explained the situation to her boyfriend and told him emphatically what she planned to do. He seemed relieved and agreed to pay half the cost. She then called her mother and asked to borrow the rest of the money for her abortion. To her surprise and relief, her mother was completely supportive.

On the day of Christy's procedure, her mother babysat while her boyfriend drove her to a clinic about an hour away. They arrived to find a waiting room filled with women from all walks of life. Put under anesthesia for the entire procedure, Christy remembers nothing about it except a tremendous surge of relief and no nausea when she woke up. She thanked everyone who helped her many times as she recovered and prepared to leave. "I am and have always been extremely thankful," she says, "and relieved that I was able to end that pregnancy and resume my life."[31]

Christy went on to graduate and received a job offer that exceeded her expectations. A short time later her boyfriend proposed, and she and her son, now in preschool, are looking forward to their new life together. Christy is grateful for the chance. "I do not regret the abortion, it was clearly the best choice I have ever made and been allowed to make in my life."[32]

An Adopted Perspective

Because Holly was adopted at eleven days old, she views the abortion debate from an entirely different angle. She is grateful her biological mother chose not to abort her, even though she knows it was a legal option at the time. Although Holly has never met her mother, she knows enough about the circumstances to guess she is the result of a spring break conception. She realizes carrying a baby to term must have been a huge sacrifice for her

Pro-life advocates tout adoption as a compassionate choice for women facing unplanned pregnancies.

It's A Girl!

ADOPTION: The Loving Option

birth mother, since it is likely the decision interrupted her education. "If my biological mother had decided to abort me," she observes, "I wouldn't be here now and I would never have had the chance to be a part of my wonderful family. When I meet other people who are adopted, they say the same thing. They are glad they have families who love them now, but they are glad someone loved them enough to give them life to start with."[33]

As an adult, Holly has heard the stories of friends who made the decision to abort. For most of the people she knows, the experience has not been positive. One friend described a painful abortion experience that left her emotionally raw. A year later Holly witnessed the friend suddenly become very emotional at a party and begin crying as she expressed remorse over her abortion. While she respects the rights of others to make their own decisions, in Holly's observation "abortion is a sad thing."[34]

Reasons for Abortions

In a 2004 survey by the Guttmacher Institute, women gave the following as the primary reason for their decision to abort:

Not ready for the responsibility of a child—25 percent

Financial concerns—23 percent

Does not want more children—19 percent

Effort to avoid single parenthood—8 percent

Not mature enough for a child—7 percent

Would interfere with education or career—4 percent

Pressured by partner or parents—1 percent

Other reasons—6.5 percent

Mother's health—4 percent

Possible fetal health problems—3 percent

Rape or incest—0.5 percent

Wm. Robert Johnston, "Reasons Given for Having Abortions in the United States." www.johnstonsarchive.net/policy/abortion/abreasons.html. (www.guttmacher.org/pubs/psrh/full/3711005.pdf.)

Mixed Feelings

At eighteen Kim was a college student with no plans to marry or quit school. When faced with an unwanted pregnancy, she opted for an abortion. She was ashamed and embarrassed by the situation but never considered any other option. Her boyfriend left town shortly before she discovered she was pregnant, allowing the entire drama to play itself out before he knew anything about it.

A clinic worker shows a patient a model of the female reproductive system before her abortion. Some women credit their interactions with workers at abortion clinics with making the experience more positive.

Kim eventually told her parents, who grudgingly agreed to pay for an abortion. The procedure was performed in a doctor's office, but because she had waited so long, it was necessary to perform a surgical abortion. During the procedure Kim's cervix was dilated, which she found extremely painful. She recalls being awake through the whole thing and being able to hear the motor on a vacuum. When it was over she was determined to get on with her life and be more careful with contraceptives in the future.

By 1991 Kim was twenty-two, living on her own, and working as a caseworker for a government agency. She was in a relationship with a man she adored and expected to marry eventually, but she still was not ready for a child. When her "hit-and-miss" contraception tactics failed to keep her from getting pregnant again, she was faced with another decision. With the support of her partner, Kim again decided to abort.

British Feminist on Record

"Myself, I'd as soon weep over my taken tonsils or my absent appendix as snivel over those [five] abortions. I had a choice, and I chose life—mine." —Julie Burchill, English journalist.

Julie Burchill, "Abortion: Still a Dirty Word," *Guardian*, May 25, 2002. www.guardian. co.uk/lifeandstyle/2002/may/25/weekend.julieburchill.

This time the setting was a private clinic where the staff was very engaging from the outset. They offered information, counseling, and even suggested alternatives to abortion. When it became clear Kim's mind was made up, the staff was careful to make sure she was fully informed about her choice but did not try to dissuade her. Kim remembers nothing about the abortion itself—just that the staff was caring and helpful.

With two abortions behind her, Kim was ready to move on. "I'm a decisive person," she says. "Once I make a decision I don't slow down. I just move on from there."[35]

When Kim found herself pregnant again in 2002, however, the situation was different. She was thirty-three years old and working as a marketing manager for a cruise line. Her partner was adamant about fathering a child—he did not want one. In spite of her misgivings, Kim allowed herself to be talked into an abortion. Looking back she says: "My first two abortions left me with no regrets. I made what I thought was the best decision at the time and I was prepared to live with it. But the third one—it haunted me. I didn't want it. I didn't think it was necessary, but I did it because I was trying to save a relationship. It didn't work. I ended up resenting him for it. As it turned out—we were both emotionally devastated by it."[36]

There are many voices in the abortion debate. Some are from men or from women who have never experienced an unwanted pregnancy. Perhaps the voices that speak the loudest are those who have been there, made their decision, and have a story to tell.

THE FUTURE OF ABORTION

As participants in the abortion debate look to the future, resolutions of the current questions seem unlikely. Scientific developments and a shift in attitudes about certain kinds of abortions, however, may change the direction of the debate.

NOT IN MY FAMILY

"There are many pro-choicers who, while paying obeisance to the rights of people with disabilities, want . . . to preserve their right to ensure that no one with disabilities will be born into their own families." —Patricia Bauer, journalist and mother of a Down syndrome child.

Patricia Bauer, "The Abortion Debate No One Wants to Have," *Washington Post*, October 18, 2005. www.washingtonpost.com/wp-dyn/content/article/2005/10/17/AR2005101701311.html?referrer=emailarticle.

Selective Abortions

Most of the abortions now being performed in the United States occur because the pregnancy is unplanned and having a child would create financial or emotional hardship for the mother. Another, much smaller, percentage are therapeutic abortions that are the result of a medical condition in which allowing a pregnancy to be carried to term would likely endanger a woman's health. A third type, selective abortion, has risen sharply over the last few years.

Selective abortions are performed in cases where a particular fetus is perceived as having undesirable characteristics. This may include the absence or presence of a specific genetic property, a genetic defect, undesirable gender, or some other feature that does not appeal to the parents. In cases of multiple fetuses due to fertility treatments, selective abortion may also be used to reduce the risk to the remaining fetuses.

An activist in India protests the selective abortion of female fetuses following the establishment of clinics for sex determination.

Sex and Pregnancy Among Teens

- By their 18th birthday, six in 10 teenage women and more than five in 10 teenage men have had sexual intercourse.
- Of the approximately 750,000 teen pregnancies that occur each year, 82% are unintended. More than one-quarter end in abortion.
- The pregnancy rate among U.S. women aged 15–19 has declined steadily—from 117 pregnancies per 1,000 women in 1990 to 75 per 1,000 women in 2002.
- Approximately 14% of the decline in teen pregnancy between 1995 and 2002 was due to teens' delaying sex or having sex less often, while 86% was due to an increase in sexually experienced teens' contraceptive use.

- Despite the decline, the United States continues to have one of the highest teen pregnancy rates in the developed world—almost twice as high as those of England, Wales and Canada, and eight times as high as those of the Netherlands and Japan.
- Every year, roughly nine million new sexually transmitted infections (STIs) occur among teens and young adults in the United States. Compared with rates among teens in Canada and Western Europe, rates of gonorrhea and chlamydia among U.S. teens are extremely high.

Excerpted from Guttmacher Institute, "Facts on Sex Education in the United States," 2006. www.guttmacher.org/pubs/fb_sexEd2006.html.

In some countries where male children are considered more desirable than females, couples have taken advantage of technology to determine the sex of a child before birth. If the fetus is not the boy the parents are hoping for, many are choosing to abort. Researchers estimate around 10 million female fetuses have been aborted in India over the past two decades. Similar trends are evident in China, Afghanistan, Nepal, Pakistan, and South Korea. In a 2007 report to the United Nations, the Institute for Family Policy and eighteen other organizations estimated 100 million women are missing from today's population as a result of selective abortion or female infanticide.

New Abortion Questions

Although some cultural groups have higher occurrences of selective abortion for this purpose than others, in the United States the question of gender is less important. Because prenatal testing allows genetic defects to be detected in the womb, many fetuses that might have been born disabled prior to this technology are being aborted. Some worry that parents are being pressured by health care providers to abort in these cases, effectively eliminating an entire population of people.

Patricia Bauer, *Washington Post* reporter and the mother of a child with Down syndrome, often encounters a negative so-

A mother with a Down syndrome baby. The possibility that parents will abort children who are thought of as "less desirable" is a major issue in the abortion debate as prenatal genetic testing becomes more widespread.

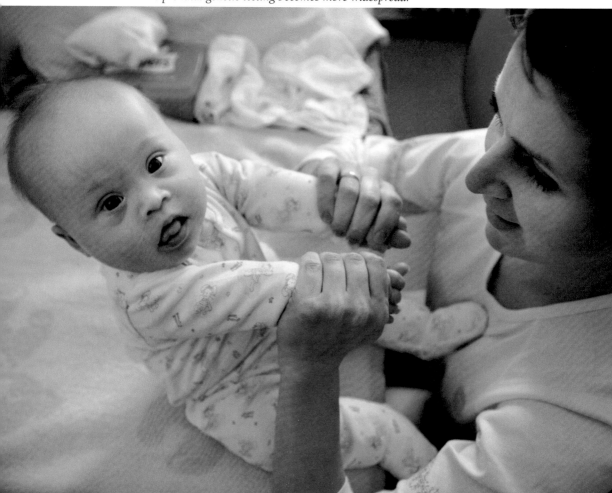

cial attitude when accompanied by her daughter. "To them, [my daughter] falls into the category of avoidable human suffering," she notes. "That someone I love is regarded in this way is unspeakably painful to me. The abortion debate is not just about a woman's right to choose whether to have a baby; it's also [becoming] about a woman's right to choose which baby she wants to have."[37]

The availability of prenatal genetic testing is changing the kinds of questions being raised by the abortion issue. The idea of being able to choose which fetuses are healthy enough or perfect enough to be born is a subject no one seems ready to tackle just yet. There are currently no guidelines to determine how serious a genetic defect must be in order to justify aborting. In the next ten to twenty years, the abortion issues that provoke the most intense debate today may disappear completely—giving way to new controversies over issues like selective abortion.

WILL WE REGRET OUR BRAVE NEW WORLD?

"Artificial wombs are different from current technologies . . . because they represent the final severing of reproduction from the human body. . . . We should remember this . . . as we expand the reach of our powers over the . . . origins of human life, lest we give birth to a technology we will live to regret." —Christine Rosen, senior editor of *New Atlantis* and a fellow at the Ethics and Public Policy Center.

Christine Rosen, "Why Not Artificial Wombs?" *New Atlantis*, Fall 2003, p. 76.

Artificial Wombs—Science Fiction or Just a Matter of Time?

Another possible agent of change in the abortion debate is the science of ectogenesis (the creation of life outside the uterus). Advances in this field have the potential to change the point at which a fetus becomes viable to a much earlier stage of pregnancy. This might one day be possible through the development of artificial wombs. The success of this work could dramatically impact abortions in the future.

Thirty years ago the world was shocked by the developments in assisted reproduction that led to the first "test tube babies." Some scientists have gone so far as to suggest another thirty years will find artificial wombs as commonplace as test tube babies are today.

Most of the current research with artificial wombs is being done by Hung-Ching Liu of Cornell University's Centre for Reproductive Medicine and Infertility. Liu has undertaken this work in an effort to help women overcome infertility. She hopes to create a womb from a woman's own endometrial cells in which an embryo could be placed and allowed to grow with no danger of organ rejection. Theoretically, this womb could be utilized from conception throughout gestational development.

Current research on the development of artificial wombs may make it possible for a fetus to develop outside of a woman's body. Such a development changes the dynamics of the abortion debate.

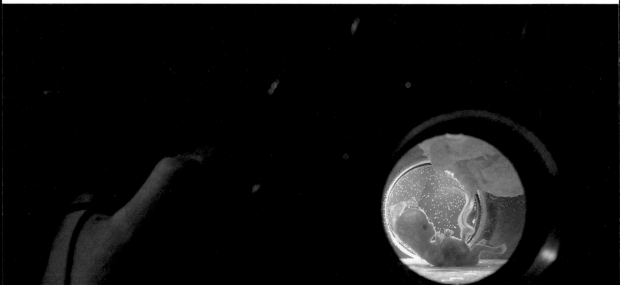

Brief History of Birth Control

1960

The FDA approves Enovid—the first birth control pill. The pill is 100 percent effective—but has terrible side effects. Eventually, it is realized that the dose is ten times too high.

1976

IUDs (intrauterine devices) are approved by the FDA. These devices are inserted by doctors and provide birth control for up to ten years. They fall out of favor after one—the Dalkon Shield—is found to cause pelvic inflammatory disease in some women.

1980s

The modern, low-dose, two- and three-phase birth control pills become available.

1992

The FDA approves the first hormone shot to prevent pregnancy for several months at a time—Depo Provera.

1998

The first emergency contraception is approved by the FDA. Women can take Preven pills up to seventy-two hours after sex to prevent pregnancy.

2000–2002

Four new birth control products are approved by the FDA. Ortho Evra, a birth control patch, slowly releases hormones through the skin. NuvaRing, a small, flexible ring, is inserted into the vagina and releases hormones for three weeks. Lunelle is a monthly hormone injection. Mirena is an IUD effective for five years.

2003

The first continuous birth control pill, Seasonale, which women take every day to suppress their periods and provide birth control, was approved in September. Seasonale schedules four menstrual periods a year.

Some pro-life supporters have seized on the idea of artificial wombs as a possible solution to the problem of unwanted pregnancies. Since most states already have restrictions on abortion after viability, they see the development of this technology as a way to extend greatly the period of viability. They argue that since it would be possible for an embryo to survive outside its mother's body, theoretically from the moment of conception, the need for abortion would be eradicated.

Alarmed by reaction to her earliest experimental results in 2001, Liu began to realize the enormous social impact her work could have. She halted her experiments for a full year in order to think through her goals and make certain decisions. "I don't want to make a womb for the convenience of women who don't want to be pregnant,"[38] she says, refusing to engage in the discussion of how her work might affect the abortion debate. "We hope to create complete artificial wombs using these techniques in a few years . . . [so that] women with damaged uteruses and wombs will be able to have babies for the first time."[39]

In spite of Liu's personal feelings about future applications of her work, artificial wombs are likely to have some effect on the future of abortions. How much can only be determined by time.

Common Ground for Now

While the influence of artificial wombs is not likely to be felt for many years, the immediate future of abortion may hinge on finding common ground. Most pro-life and pro-choice advocates can agree the root cause of abortion, at least for now, is unwanted pregnancy. No one, including most pro-choice supporters, would argue that abortion is a good solution. By working together to increase the range of possible solutions, it may be possible to reduce dramatically the number of unwanted pregnancies that end in abortion.

In the 1990s an organization called the Common Ground Network for Life and Choice made an effort to identify areas of overlapping concern (and agreement) to both sides of the abortion debate. Some of their discussions focused on preventing teen pregnancy, making adoption a more accessible choice, and increasing options for women. The Common Ground approach encouraged pro-life and pro-choice supporters to spend less time engaged in debate and more time combining their efforts to achieve shared goals. By the late 1990s, however, the lack of public focus on the abortion question along with the loss of most of their funding brought an end to the group. In spite of this, their goal of focusing on shared concerns and common ground is a worthwhile approach for the future.

ABORTION DEBATE RENDERED OBSOLETE?

"The pro-life versus pro-choice debate seems to be destined for a short lifespan. It is likely that abortion will largely disappear in this country during the 21st century—not because it has been banned, but simply because it has been rendered obsolete." —Tom Head, civil liberties author for About.com.

Tom Head, "Pro-Life vs. Pro-Choice," About.com: Civil Liberties. http://civilliberty.about.com/od/abortion/tp/Pro-Life-vs-Pro-Choice.htm.

Sex Education

One of the areas identified by both pro-life and pro-choice groups as common ground is the need for better sex education. A few years ago efforts to introduce comprehensive sex education in schools met with resistance, but recent polls show a shift in attitude. Today more than 90 percent of Americans agree sex education should be taught in schools.

While most everyone agrees sex education programs are a good idea, how far this education should go is still a topic of debate. A 2004 NPR/Kaiser/Kennedy School poll shows 46 percent favor an "abstinence-plus" approach. This means teaching teens that abstinence is best, but includes information about condoms, contraception, and making responsible decisions about sex at a minimum. A more comprehensive sex education course might also cover family planning, reproduction, body image, sexual values, dating and relationships, communication and negotiation skills, and sexually transmitted infections (STIs) and how to avoid them, in addition to basic contraception.

Current research shows failure to address teen sexuality leads to higher incidences of STIs and teenage pregnancy. In countries where comprehensive sex education programs are in place, the rates are much lower. The 2002 teen pregnancy rate in the United States, for example, was about seventy-five per one thousand women aged fifteen to nineteen compared with less than ten per one thousand in the Netherlands, where more comprehensive sex education programs are the norm. As Heather Boonstra, a Guttmacher senior public policy associate,

A teacher gives a lecture on sex education to a group of high school girls. Both the pro-life and pro-choice camps believe that better sex education will help reduce the number of abortions.

points out: "Comprehensive sex education stresses abstinence and responsible decision making, but also includes information on contraception and avoiding sexually transmitted infections. Both the evidence and the American public strongly support using this approach to help young people transition from adolescence to adulthood safely and responsibly."[40]

Published in 2007, the results of a nine-year study commissioned by Congress and conducted by Mathematica Policy Research show abstinence-only programs are no more likely to influence teens to delay sexual initiation than the more comprehensive counterparts and may actually increase unplanned pregnancies. Given these results, new sex education classes are likely to include a wider range of topics as parents, schools, and government agencies consider the effectiveness of future programs.

An obvious, but often overlooked, source of information about what sex education should cover is the teens the programs are supposed to address. When asked, teens have suggested less emphasis on anatomy and scare tactics and more discussion of negotiation in sexual relationships as well as basic communication skills. They also suggest that information about health clinics should be highly visible in places young people frequent, such as shopping centers, school restrooms, and theaters.

Better sex education programs are a common goal for most pro-life and pro-choice groups—when they can reach agreement about the content. As efforts are made to work together to create more effective programs, both sides hope to reduce the number of unwanted pregnancies and ultimately the number of abortions.

Birth Control in the Twenty-first Century

The majority of Americans believe a key component of an effective sex education program is information about methods of birth control. But one barrier to more cooperation between pro-life and pro-choice groups is their disagreement about which methods of birth control are actually contraceptive in nature— that is, they prevent conception.

Most pro-life advocates believe any birth control method that may allow fertilization of an egg is actually an abortifacient (causes the termination of a pregnancy). Some argue these types of birth control (which include most hormonal contraceptives such as the pill, the Minipill, Depo-Provera, and Norplant) should not be categorized as contraception and would not include them in sex education programs. Pro-choice supporters, however, believe pregnancy does not begin until implantation. They see the exclusion of these birth control options as severely limiting.

Recent polls conducted by the American Pregnancy Organization and Ortho Pharmaceutical Corporation both show most Americans prefer the pill as their primary means of birth control. Condoms are the second-most preferred method and are sometimes used along with the pill. As advances in birth control techniques continue, however, new options may soon be available.

BOYS ON THE PILL

"What if it became common practice for 16-year-old boys to talk to their fathers about getting 'that prescription,' just as many girls do with their mothers? Maybe young men might even start viewing sex in a more serious, responsible light." —Alex Mar, editor *Rolling Stone*.

Alex Mar, "Jagged Little Pill: Will Male Birth Control Ever Become a Reality?" *Slate.com*, October 1, 2004. http://slate.com/id/2107558.

A promising male contraceptive that would render sperm unable to fertilize an egg is undergoing trials. One injection could last up to ten years and appears to have no unpleasant side effects. The method is currently being tested in India and may be available soon.

Hormonal methods for men are also in development and could be available in the next five to ten years. Getting the dosage right is a challenge, and the side effects are similar to those felt by some female pill users. By interfering with the production of sperm, these methods would prevent the fertilization of eggs—an acceptable contraceptive for pro-life supporters.

Fertility computers are handheld devices that calculate the days a woman is ovulating. Although not currently available in

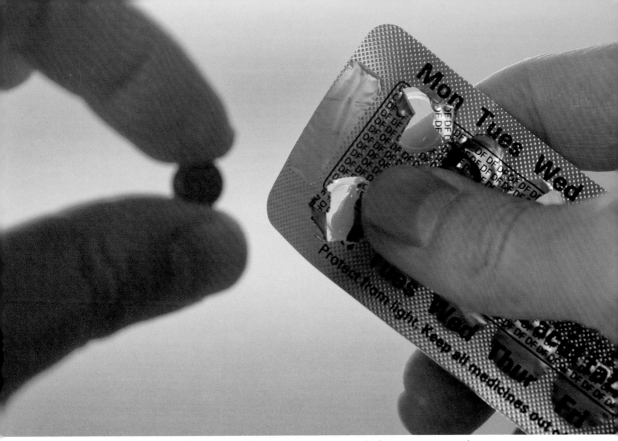

Birth control pills continue to be the preferred method of contraception in the twenty-first century.

the United States, they are expected to be approved by the FDA in the near future. They are likely to be used as both birth control and a fertility aid.

The Adoption Option

Pro-life and pro-choice organizations have a common goal of making abortion a rare occurrence. Many people from both sides of the debate tout adoption as a positive solution once an unwanted pregnancy is discovered. Pro-life supporters, in particular, believe adoption is the best alternative to abortion and a more responsible choice. While they recognize carrying a baby to term is inconvenient and uncomfortable for the mother, they believe adoption is choosing what is best for the unborn.

Some pro-choice supporters are uncomfortable with adoption, but others see it as a viable option as long as it is not forced. They believe the various degrees of the open adoptions of today make it a more attractive solution than it has been in the past, but they argue that increased social supports and appropriate counseling are necessary to make it successful. Many pro-choice advocates point out they are in favor of any reproductive choice a woman makes—whether it is abortion, keeping her child, or placing her child for adoption.

New Legislation on the Horizon?

There are, however, new challenges to the efforts to find common ground in the abortion debate. First introduced to Congress in 2004 by Senator Barbara Boxer, the Freedom of Choice Act, or FOCA, sought to establish abortion rights as part of a woman's civil liberties. The original bill called a woman's decision to begin, continue, prevent, or terminate a pregnancy a private one that should be free of government interference. Its purpose was to remove all barriers to a full range of reproductive services and nullify any state or federal laws previously enacted to control them.

In 2004 the bill was presented to the 108th Congress and then sent to a committee without reaching a vote. During the 2008 presidential campaign, however, then candidate Barack Obama assured supporters he would sign the bill into law if passed by Congress. In January 2009, as the 111th Congress began its session, the FOCA is set to make a comeback to the congressional floor. Due to shifting party majorities in Congress, passage of the bill is possible if it reaches a vote. In this case the battle lines would immediately be redrawn and a lengthy fight is likely to ensue.

As the twenty-first century unfolds, the abortion debate that has been raging for over thirty-five years seems destined to continue. The questions coming out of this debate have polarized the nation and created two very different schools of thought. While it is unlikely opinions about abortion will change, it could be that the political outcome of this debate may well be overridden by the medical and scientific advances of the future.

NOTES

Chapter 1: Is Abortion Moral?

1. Quoted in "When Does Life Begin," AllAboutPopularIssues.org. www.allaboutpopularissues.org/when-does-life-begin-faq.htm.

2. Association of Prolife Physicians, "What About the Morning-After Pill?" www.prolifephysicians.org/map_esc.htm.

3. Joyce Arthur, "What Pro-Choice Really Means." http://mypage. direct.ca/w/writer/realchoice.html.

4. Hillary Clinton, speech at NARAL, Washington, DC, January 22, 1999. www.ontheissues.org/Senate/Hillary_Clinton_ Abortion.htm.

5. Margaret Sykes, "Abortion—Pro Choice Views," AllExperts.com. http://en.allexperts.com/q/Abortion-Pro-Choice-338/Parental-involvement-laws-teen.htm.

6. George Monbiot, "Face Facts, Cardinal. Our Awful Rate of Abortion Is Partly Your Responsibility," *Guardian* (Manchester), February 26, 2008, p. 33.

7. Quoted in ThinkExist.com, "Michael J. Tucker Quotes." http://thinkexist.com/quotes/michael_j._tucker.

8. Peter Singer and Helen Kuhse, "On Letting Handicapped Infants Die," in James Rachels, ed., *The Right Thing to Do: Basic Readings in Moral Philosophy*. New York: Random House, 1989, p. 146.

9. C. Everett Koop and Timothy Johnson, *Let's Talk*. Grand Rapids, MI: Zondervan, 1992, p. 21.

10. Anna Quindlen, *Living Out Loud*. New York: Random House, 1988, p. 210.

Chapter 2: Is Abortion a Constitutional Right?

11. Quoted in Mark Harding, *Early Christian Life and Thought in Social Context*. Sheffield, England: Sheffield Academic Press, 2003, p. 264.

12. James Wilson, *The Works of the Honorable James Wilson, L.L.D.*, Vol. 2, Ch. 12, 1804, www.constitution.org/jwilson/jwilson.htm.

13. Report, Committee on the Judiciary, U.S. Senate, on Senate Joint Resolution 3, 98th Congress, 98-149, June 7, 1983, p. 6.

14. Quoted in FindLaw, "U.S. Supreme Court, *Roe v. Wade*, 410 U.S. 113, 1973." http://caselaw.lp.findlaw.com/scripts/getcase.pl?court=US&vol=410&invol=113.

15. Quoted in About.com: Women's History, "*Roe v. Wade* Supreme Court Decision." http://womenshistory.about.com/library/etext/gov/bl_roe_m.htm.

16. Ronald Reagan, *Abortion and the Conscience of the Nation.* New York: Thomas Nelson, Human Life Foundation, 1984, p. 16.

17. Quoted in Guttmacher Institute, "An Overview of Abortion in the United States." www.guttmacher.org/media/presskits/2005/06/28/abortionoverview.html.

Chapter 3: More Abortion Questions

18. Quoted in ReligiousTolerance.org, "D & X/PBA Procedures: Introduction." www.religioustolerance.org/abo_pba1.htm.

19. Quoted in John Leo, "Anti-Abortion Viewpoints Absent from Most Media," *Seattle Times*. http://community.seattletimes.nwsource.com/archive/?date=19960604&slug=2332714.

20. Sykes, "Abortion."

Chapter 4: Does Abortion Have Long-Term Effects?

21. American Cancer Society, "Can Having an Abortion Cause or Contribute to Breast Cancer?": Cancer Reference Information, August 11, 2008. www.cancer.org/docroot/CRI/content/CRI_2_6x_Can_Having_an_Abortion_Cause_or_Contribute_to_Breast_Cancer.asp.

22. John M. Thorp Jr., Katherine E. Hartmann, and Elizabeth Shadigian, "Long-Term Physical and Psychological Health Consequences of Induced Abortion," *Obstetrical and Gynecological Survey*, 2003.

23. Quoted in Guttmacher Institute, *Abortion in Women's Lives*, 2006, p. 24. www.guttmacher.org/pubs/2006/05/04/AiWL.pdf.

24. Susan Cohen, "Abortion and Mental Health: Myths and Re-alities," *Guttmacher Policy Review*, Summer 2006. www.guttm acher.org/pubs/gpr/09/3/gpr090308.html.

25. Quoted in ReligiousTolerance.org, "Post-Abortion Syndrome: Who Are Vulnerable?" www.religioustolerance.org/abo_post1. htm.

Chapter 5: Voices of Experience

26. Barbara B., interview with author, Houston, Texas, June 2008.

27. Quoted in I'm Not Sorry.net, "Alexandra's Story." www.im notsorry.net/alexandra.htm.

28. Deborah A., telephone interview with author, August 2008.

29. Deborah A., August 2008.

30. Quoted in I'm Not Sorry.net, "Christy's Story." www.imnot sorry.net/christyA.htm.

31. Quoted in I'm Not Sorry.net, "Christy's Story."

32. Quoted in I'm Not Sorry.net, "Christy's Story."

33. Holly L., Internet interview with author, July 2008.

34. Holly L., July 2008.

35. Kim C., telephone interview with author, August 2008.

36. Kim C., August 2008.

Chapter 6: The Future of Abortion

37. Patricia Bauer, "The Abortion Debate No One Wants to Have," *Washington Post*, October 18, 2005. www.washingtonpost.com/ wp-dyn/content/article/2005/10/17/AR2005101701311. html?referrer=emailarticle.

38. Quoted in *Popular Science*, "Artificial Wombs." www.popsci. com/scitech/article/2005-08/artificial-wombs.

39. Quoted in *Guardian*, "Men Redundant? Now We Don't Need Women Either." www.guardian.co.uk/world/2002/feb/10/ medicalscience.research.

40. Quoted in Guttmacher Institute, "Strong Evidence Favors Comprehensive Approach to Sex Ed." www.guttmacher. org/media/nr/2007/05/23/index.html.

DISCUSSION QUESTIONS

Chapter 1: Is Abortion Moral?

1. According to recent polls, how does the American public generally feel about the morality of abortion?

2. What conflict exists between America's public and private feelings about abortion?

3. What are your feelings about the morality of abortion? How did you arrive at your conclusion?

Chapter 2: Is Abortion a Constitutional Right?

1. What is the significance of the *Roe v. Wade* decision of 1973?

2. Upon what part (or parts) of the Constitution did the Supreme Court base its decision?

3. Do you believe abortion is a right guaranteed by the Constitution? Why or why not?

Chapter 3: More Abortion Questions

1. What is a late-term abortion, and why are some people opposed to it as an abortion option?

2. How do parental consent and notification laws affect minors? What other options are available in states that have these types of laws?

3. Do you believe parental notification laws are appropriate? Why or why not?

Chapter 4: Does Abortion Have Long-Term Effects?

1. What (if any) long-term effects have researchers determined are connected to abortion?

2. What are the difficulties with abortion studies, and how does this affect how the results are interpreted?

3. What sources of information would you assume are the most reliable when it comes to the topic of abortion and why?

Chapter 5: Voices of Experience

1. What were some of the factors that led women in these stories to consider abortion?

2. Did any of the stories allow you to see an aspect of abortion you had not considered? Which one and why?

3. Based on what you know about abortion, if you or someone you know was facing an unwanted pregnancy, how would you advise them?

Chapter 6: The Future of Abortion

1. According to the author, what is likely to be the biggest moral and ethical question related to abortion in the future?

2. What scientific discoveries may make it possible for a fetus to reach full term outside its mother's body? How will this affect abortion in the future?

3. Which birth control methods of the future do you find to be the most attractive and why?

ORGANIZATIONS TO CONTACT

American Life League
PO Box 1350
Stafford, VA 22555
Phone: (540) 659-4171
Fax: (540) 659-2586
E-mail: info@all.org
Web site: www.all.org

American Life League is an organization that was cofounded in 1979 by Judie Brown. It is the largest grassroots Catholic pro-life organization in the United States and is committed to the protection of all innocent human beings from the moment of creation to natural death.

National Abortion and Reproductive
Rights Action League (NARAL)
1156 Fifteenth St. NW, Suite 700
Washington, DC 20005
Phone: (202) 973-3000
Fax: (202) 973-3096
Web site: www.prochoiceamerica.org

NARAL Pro-Choice America is committed to protecting the right to choose and electing candidates who will promote policies to prevent unintended pregnancy.

National Right to Life Committee (NRLC)
512 Tenth St. NW
Washington, DC 20004
Phone: (202) 626-8800
E-mail: nrcl@nrlc.org
Web site: www.nrlc.org

The ultimate goal of the National Right to Life Committee is to restore legal protection to innocent human life. It is also concerned with related matters of medical ethics that relate to the right-to-life issues of euthanasia and infanticide. The committee does not have a position on issues such as contraception, sex education, capital punishment, and national defense.

Operation Rescue
PO Box 782888
Wichita, KS 67278-2888
Phone: (316) 683-6790
Toll free: (800) 705-1175
Fax: (316) 244-2636
E-mail: info@operationrescue.org
Web site: www.operationrescue.org

Operation Rescue is the leading pro-life Christian activist organization in the nation. Its activities are on the cutting edge of the abortion issue, taking direct action to restore legal personhood to the unborn and stop abortion.

Physicians for Reproductive Choice and Health (PRCH)
55 W. Thirty-ninth St., Suite 1001
New York, NY 10018-3889
Phone: (646) 366-1890
Fax: (646) 366-1897
E-mail: info@prch.org
Web site: www.prch.org

PRCH exists to ensure that all people have the knowledge, access to quality services, and freedom to make their own reproductive health decisions. PRCH mobilizes pro-choice physicians to promote, educate, and advocate about the importance of comprehensive reproductive health care.

Planned Parenthood Federation of America (PPFA)
434 W. Thirty-third St.
New York, NY 10001
Phone: (212) 541-7800
Fax: (212) 245-1845
Web site: www.plannedparenthood.org

PPFA provides health care services, sex education, and sexual health information to millions of women, men, and young people. For more than ninety years, Planned Parenthood has promoted a commonsense approach to women's health and well-being based on respect for each individual's right to make informed, independent decisions about sex, health, and family planning.

Pregnancy Centers (Option Line)
Phone: (800) 395-4357
Web site: www.pregnancycenters.org

This pro-life organization's Option Line consultants refer callers to pregnancy resource centers in their area for answers to questions about abortion, pregnancy tests, STIs, adoption, parenting, medical referrals, housing, and many other issues. The toll-free number is available to callers twenty-four hours a day, seven days a week.

FOR MORE INFORMATION

Books

Gloria Feldt, *Behind Every Choice Is a Story*. Denton: University of North Texas Press/Planned Parenthood Federation of America, 2002. A pro-choice discussion of unwanted pregnancy options interwoven with personal stories.

Barbar Horak, *Real Abortion Stories: The Hurting and the Healing*. El Paso, TX: Strive for the Best, 2007. First-person accounts of abortion and the circumstances that led to the decision to abort.

Corinne J. Naden, *Abortion (Open for Debate)*. New York: Benchmark, 2007. Nonfiction overview of the abortion debate.

Auriana Ojeda, ed., *Should Abortion Rights Be Restricted?* Detroit: Greenhaven, 2002. A collection of essays about whether abortion rights should be upheld.

Christine Watkins, ed., *The Ethics of Abortion*. Detroit: Greenhaven, 2005. A collection of essays from both sides of the abortion debate related to ethics and morality.

Dorrie Williams-Wheeler, *The Unplanned Pregnancy Book for Teens and College Students*. Virginia Beach, VA: Sparkledoll Productions, 2004. A comprehensive handbook for young women, covering all aspects of pregnancy, childbearing, adoption, and abortion.

Web Sites

Abortion Access: All Sides of the Issue, ReligiousTolerance. org (www.religioustolerance.org/abortion.htm). A Web site that deals with a variety of subjects, including abortion. All viewpoints are discussed, including the full spectrum of pro-life beliefs and the full diversity of pro-choice beliefs.

The Abortion Debate, Quickoverview.com (www.quickover view.com/issues/abortion-debate.html). In keeping with the spirit of the Internet, QuickOverview.com is an exchange of ideas by experts in specific subject matters. This article is an interesting and unbiased discussion of the topic of abortion.

Alan Guttmacher Institute (www.guttmacher.org). The Gutt-macher Institute is known for its research in the field of reproductive health. Although pro-choice in philosophy, the data provided by the Guttmacher Institute are generally considered reliable by both pro-choice and pro-life organizations.

ProLife.com (www.prolife.com). All things pro-life, including videos, books, articles, blogs, and pregnancy information.

INDEX

PICTURE CREDITS

ABOUT THE AUTHOR

Wendy Lanier is an author, teacher, and speaker who writes and speaks on a variety of topics related to children and parenting. She is married to a college professor and is the mother of two daughters.